Leslie Gore

Annie Jennings
A novel. Part 3

ISBN/EAN: 9783337065645

Printed in Europe, USA, Canada, Australia, Japan

Cover: Foto ©Andreas Hilbeck / pixelio.de

More available books at **www.hansebooks.com**

Leslie Gore

Annie Jennings

A novel. Part 3

ANNIE JENNINGS.

A Novel.

BY

LESLIE GORE.

IN THREE VOLUMES.
VOL. III.

LONDON:
RICHARD BENTLEY, NEW BURLINGTON STREET.
1870.

CONTENTS

OF

THE THIRD VOLUME.

CHAPTER I.

PENELOPE MEETS STRANGERS QUITE
UNEXPECTEDLY.

BEES CRAG the residence of the
Reverend Mr. Elliot, was a pic-
turesquely situated place on a rising
ground, and commanded a splendid
view of the upper end of Loch Achray.
The house was a square solid build-
ing, of the dark gray stone of the
country, whose colour contrasted

VOL. III.   B

pleasantly with luxuriant creeping plants artfully trained up its sides by Mr. Elliot, who was a famous gardener. To the very roofs trailed up these creepers, fastened to slender wires, placed at regular distances, forming a lattice pattern, and by careful clipping this leafy framework was kept in due bounds. At the back of this pretty flowering abode were laid out terrace gardens, sloping down to the loch's cool sides. These beds were now in brilliant beauty, scarlet, and red, and yellow dazzling the eye, and intoxicating the restless bees that knew not which to prefer, the sweets of the cultivated garden's flowers, or the heather, not yet deepened into its purple beauty. Mr. Elliot was proud of his hives, and made a despot over them—himself quite scathless—dressed in a gauze robe and with large gloves, when he made inroads on their dominions as he pleased, and stole their stored treasures as he willed.

Bees Crag was quite as dear to Penelope as Lunar Lodge, and was nearly as much her home; was it not Billie's home? then it must be hers also; and Mr. and Mrs. Elliot were very fond of the gay little girl.

Penelope had not written to Billie apprising him of the day they were to be home, and on the morning after their arrival she paddled herself up the loch, like any Lady of the Lake, to the foot of Bees Crag.

Quite under the garden cliff was the Elliots' little boat-house, into this she now ran her boat, fastened it, and tripping up the stairs found, as she expected, the wicket unlocked. Along the terrace walk she ran eagerly, so as to escape notice, wishing to burst in unexpectedly on Mr. and Mrs. Elliot and Billie, at breakfast. She knew their breakfast hour was rather a late one, and very late compared to theirs at home; so she thought to catch them all together, and to be smothered at once with kisses and welcomes, and another breakfast to be pressed on her whether she would or no, by kind dear Mrs. Elliot. And the fresh mountain air made her think rather complacently of the cream and honey and homemade bread in prospect.

But what anticipations are ever realized? From the most trivial of them up to the greatest, they are never quite as we expect, and never once quite the same again. Once before Penelope had made a raid on Bees Crag, found them at breakfast, and ate a second breakfast, so now she thought to do so again. One more turn she has to take and then she will reach the conservatory door, through which she means to creep, and get at the morning room just beyond it.

A bower covered with clematis and honeysuckle lies here, and from its thickly shaded covering, she hears men's voices—strange voices. Penelope starts ; can there be company and Billie not to tell her ? True she had not answered his last two letters—the last reaching her a fortnight back. Penelope is a little shy from want of meeting with society, except old Mr. and Mrs. Elliot's, and the boy Billie's, not shy from native timidity. She steps behind a chesnut tree to make quite sure before advancing another step, and now she hears unmistakably a stranger's voice—a sweet low clear voice — very — very — melodious Miss Penelope at once decided it was, and *so* manly. She crimsons with a new pleasure and looks all unconsciously very pretty, as she leans forward from behind the tree, yet still in shadow. Her large straw hat suspended from her arm, is tied with a blue bow, and her rich waving hair falls on her ivory throat. Now she hears another voice louder than the first, not so sweet she thinks, but deep and manly also, and a phrase she catches—

" Charley, I think it was a risk you ran, bringing that delicate child such a distance and in the night air. Could you not have staid quietly in Edinburgh last night, and have come on here to-day? Time enough, one would think, but you are so restless; once Mrs. Elliot said she would be glad to have the child, she must be got here directly."

" Well, George, it was a question to be decided at once, whether I should accept the invitation for Raby and myself, we couldn't be separated; you see how she works herself into a fever if we part for half a day. As for me, I do not know that I should be here at all. Yesterday, on my way to Callander, I met—no matter—I won't tell you now, perhaps not at all."

Penelope now knows clearly that the Elliots have company, and that two gentlemen are talking in that bower—more she does not know; she does not understand their conversation, but she is aware she should not listen all the same. Oh that she could see the first speaker! and she wonders, with a young girl's awakening consciousness, what he is like. Is he young and handsome? With such a voice he must be both young and handsome; oh, that he would emerge from that tantalizing bower, too well constructed a bower by far, she thinks. Will he speak again? And with parted lips and a soft fore-finger placed on them, as if to secure their silence, she leans still further forward and again listens as that melodious voice speaks.

" Georgie, is Dr. Jennings dying ?"

The lips forget their present office at this cruel question, and with difficulty the poor girl repressed a scream ; a sound did escape, however, and Major Maitland rising, said to George Elliot, whose reply was checked by Penelope's half smothered " Oh"—

" Did you hear a child's voice ?— Could it be my little girl, I wonder ?" And instantly he walked out of the bower, cigar in mouth, and saw Penelope's excited and now tearful face.

"Hey, George, I did not know before that your father fostered Dryads; he shows good taste, I confess. Nymph," he continued, addressing Penelope, whose distress was checked by an apparition exceeding her imagination's picture—"Nymph, may a mortal approach thee unreproved ?"

"Charley, you alarm the young lady," George Elliot said, advancing with a smile, as he remarked Penelope's cheeks glow, and her eyes sought and left the ground by turns. Too shy to move, she stood facing Major Maitland until the tears grew to larger beads, then dropped in heavy rain; he mockingly bent to her his knee, saying—

"Nymph may I thus adore thee?" and kissed her drooping hand.

This finished Penelope's confusion, and gave motion to her feet that had seemed weighted to the spot. She turned and fled, whither she did not know—up—up the hill, away from the house—away from that mocking, handsome man, who knew her father and said he was dying.

She was stopped in her uncertain course by Billie, her friend Billie, who ran to meet her, scarcely able to believe the tale his eyes told him that it was indeed she.

"Penelope, dear—dear Penelope, can it be you, and where are you going,

and what has happened ? Crying ? Nay,
Penelope, tell me all about it, do not
turn aside—sit down here on this bank.
You are frightened; oh, how your
breath comes and goes so quick; sit,
dearest Pen, and rest."

Billie knelt before her, caressed and
patted her hands, told her how charmed
he was to meet her, that he had been
fearing something very bad must be
the cause of her not having written to
him for so long.

"And I had so much to tell you,
dear Pen, about ourselves here; this
very day I thought to write to you
again, but this is so much better.
When you can speak, tell me how is
Dr. Jennings; uncle told me that Dr.
M'Evoy reports favourably of him, and

the papers give excellent accounts."

"Oh, does Dr. M'Evoy say so to Mr. Elliot?" sobbed Penelope at last. "Then it is all a mistake what I heard just now."

"Ah, my poor Pen, now I understand your fright; somebody has been telling you bad stories of him. But where were you running, and from whom?"

Penelope's dimples returned, and she smiled at the question.

"There, you are all right," sighed Billie, relieved. "You will tell me your story in time, and now I will tell you mine. Look at my basket of mushrooms. I was over the moor gathering them for mother. Oh, Penelope, she is here at home with us; only think, my dear mother whom I have not seen for nine years ?"

"Your mother, Billie—Lady Julia !" ejaculated Penelope, who was becoming quite comfortable, and prepared to be interested; she would now surely hear who is the handsome stranger, and she hopes fervently he is not Colonel Elliot.

"Well, Billie, go on with your wonderful news. Did you expect her ?"

"Oh, not so soon. The last Indian mail, *viâ* Marseilles, was lost; by it Colonel Elliot had written to say they were actually *en route*. Mother and he decided all in a hurry to retire, and live at home the rest of their days. And I am so happy, it is so delightful to have a mother, and she is very—very kind and fond of me."

Poor Billie's own sweet, clinging nature made everyone seem kind to him, even those who were not kind in nature ; and Lady Julia was pleased at the boy's adoration, and at his utter unconsciousness of her having a flaw.

"Billie, I am very glad, indeed, for your sake. Billie (with hesitation, and a conscious turning aside of her face), have you any other guests ? What is Colonel Elliot like ? You have not mentioned him yet."

"Colonel Elliot is a handsome dark man (Penelope started), with very broad shoulders for his size, he is rather short (Penelope breathed easier),

and with such a good-natured manner;
oh, I am so fond of him."

"Well," · rather impatiently, said
Penelope, tapping her feet on the
stunted grass, "any more company?"

"Yes, there is his friend, Major
Maitland."—"Ah!"—(Penelope opened
her eyes wide), "such a splendid looking
fellow—a soldier, as one reads of, tall
and very handsome, and his voice, the
tone of it is lovely, but—but—some
way I don't know—I believe the fact
is I am half afraid of him."

"Afraid!" echoed Penelope, looking
down on Billie, with a slight touch of
scorn in her voice.

"Yes," he answered stoutly, "his
countenance is not agreeable, and his
manner is scoffing—light, without being

bright, and his words seem to have a double meaning always—always, do I say? and he has not been here for more than a day and a half. Yesterday he left us to fetch his child whom he had left in Edinburgh, and he returned only about two hours ago."

" A child, Billie? Is he then married?" Penelope inquired, in a tone of the deepest dejection, startling even to Billie's unawakened ear, and he asks—

" Why should you be surprised, Pen? Do you know anything about him ?"

To this query she vouchsafed no reply, then told Billie all about her father's recovery, and their return only yesterday to Lunar Lodge.

"' And Billie, it is well you have

me here—better than you think, for we were nearly spilt on the road; mother and I came on the Trossach coach, and we were met in that very narrowest bit of the road by a carriage—"

Suddenly she stopped in her relation, and colouring said—

"Now I have it, Billie—M'Alister told me that the carriage belonged to Mr. Elliot, the gentleman who ran us down was Major Maitland."

"I did not hear of this before, Pen, but if you did meet uncle's carriage yesterday with a gentleman in it, he was sure to be Major Maitland; come back to the house, for you see the morning advances, and mother will be soon ready for her mushrooms; she don't breakfast—her second breakfast, I mean—until between ten and eleven, and it is now past ten o'clock."

Slowly Penelope descended the hill with Billie, half afraid yet half anxious to meet this splendid Major; and very, very disappointed she was when she did not meet him. No appearance was there of him, nor even of Colonel Elliot. Lady Julia was still invisible, except to Billie, and the house was still and quiet, as if for an afternoon siesta, purposely so, indeed—Mrs. Elliot informed her—because of the stranger, Major Maitland's little girl.

Mrs. Elliot embraced Penelope with the affection she always manifested towards her, but somehow Penelope felt a chill—everything was so different to what she had anticipated. Mrs. Elliot was pre-occupied; her guests—and especially this new child—were engaging her attention, and she was not needed to make a brightness or variety in the house. There was no vacant place waiting for her to occupy, and poor Penelope felt saddened—except for the one brilliant interlude—the meeting with Major Maitland, and she announced that she must return home.

"I have not seen papa to-day; I heard he had a good night, but I came out too early to visit him beforehand."

"Very well, little Chestnut Blossom," answered Mrs. Elliot, and kissed her. "We must see you soon again; it is as well to keep the house quiet now on account of this poor little baby—sweet little creature, heaven bless her! Billie, I suppose you will row Pen back, and bring me word how the Doctor continues—kind compliments to him and Mrs. Jennings—bye-bye." So saying, Mrs. Elliot bustled out of the room.

" Come, Pen," said Billie, taking her hand gently with intuitive quickness, perceiving her dejection, " come, we shall have a splendid row back, I dare say you were a jolly good time pulling here this morning ?"

CHAPTER II.

PENELOPE did not feel in a good
humour—she was jealous—unconsciously jealous of this unseen child. What a
pity that Major Maitland should be
married in the first instance, and then
that he should have this child, in whom
Mrs. Elliot seemed so interested; and
Bees Crag, her second home, turned
into a convalascent hospital for this
unknown infant, or growing girl, or
whatever she was. How disagreable!

Penelope grumbled in mind, and was not as agreeable a companion as Billie desired. Suddenly she broke the silent fit she had been seized with, to ask—" Billie, where is Mrs. Maitland ?"

" I don't know," he answered, colouring to his ears; and bending low, he pulled so vigorously, as to make the boat leap, with a long stretch, forward.

" You don't know—how very odd !"

" I rather think there is no Mrs. Maitland."

" Oh, I see, he is a widower !" After a pause, Penelope asked—" How old is the girl ?"

" I don't know exactly; Raby they call her, she looks about seven or eight I should say; she is very tall and slender, and, Penelope, you must admire her, she has the loveliest face I ever saw."

Penelope's eyes danced with annoyance and passion. "Indeed! are you an admirer of her's already? I wonder you left her in her baby slumbers. Why did you not remain and watch over her with Mrs. Elliot, and the rest of them?"

"Penelope, dear, what do you mean—what are you thinking of—I do not understand you this morning?" and Billie looked rather mournfully.

Penelope put on an appearance of indifference—an indifference far from being felt, and sang in provoking fashion—

"A soldier lad I'll marry,
  And brighten his spurs so bright,
He'll call me his winsome Mary,
  His darling, his heart's delight;
I'll hold his charger's bridle,
  He'll spring to the saddle bow,
Snatch a flow'r ere we part from my girdle,
  And bless me so tender and low."

"That is bad rhyme and bad sense, Penelope, I wonder Clary sings such songs," foolishly for his own peace, said Billie, for Penelope flew at him like a young tigress.

"What do you mean by *bad* sense. I know of *non*sense, which, I suppose, means no sense, otherwise folly, but bad sense—"

"Yes, bad sense, such thoughts which produce such songs, are an evidence of bad sense."

"Absurd," drawled Penelope with a curl of her lip. "And as to Clary singing such songs, she is rather old for singing about soldiers, she leaves soldiers for young girls like me—'Yes, a soldier lad I'll marry,'" she hummed again.

But Billie was now prudently silent, and they landed at Lunar Lodge, looking wondrously grave for such young creatures ; Billie just remained to inquire for Doctor Jennings, and when told he was better, he turned to leave, merely raising his cap to Penelope.

Penelope nearly let him go, but her better nature prevailed, and catching him by the sleeve, she said, " Billie, you are a silly boy to mind my humours so. I did not mean to vex you—there now,

let us make it up—kiss and be friends,"
and she turned her fair, round cheek to
the boy's glowing lips.

Billie barely touched it, he thought it
too sacred almost to be breathed on,
and darting from her after that timid
caress, he ran until he had secured a
quiet seat among the copse wood
bordering the loch, where he sat
down to meditate over this, his first
kiss.

Pure-minded true young Billie, so
you meditated, while Penelope with a
pale face, and unhurried pulses, walked
into her father's presence.

"Papa, darling, how are you?"

Reclining on a sofa, lay Doctor Jennings, looking peaceful, yet with evidently unstrung nerves. Alas! no

nervous patient could now look into the kind firm face of the *knowing* physician (as the Scotch people say), and find comfort there; he lacked physical power, yet in unwishfulness and content, he found a peace. The oriel window, by side of which his couch was drawn, admitted a full view of the loch and the glorious pile of dark mountain forming its background. Huge Ben-venue looked down on him, with its forest of trees : the ash and oak clinging well content to its rugged sides, while the pine, more ambitious still, mounted to its very peak, and threw out branches to the sky. Doctor Jennings was a passionate lover of flowers, and delighted to be surrounded by them; now his apartment was almost too richly scented with their sweet perfume; verbenas, heliotropes, mignonette, breathed around, and clematis, jasmine, and honeysuckle, thrust in their pretty blossoms at the open window, as it were courting the notice of the sick man. Still dearer to him than the garden flowers, were their wild relations of the woods, and in rustic baskets of various pretty shapes lay the primrose in its green leaves, and that sweetest of all perfumes, the violet.

"Well, my Queen," said the Doctor smiling, holding her from him to inspect her the better, "how is Ulysses?"

"Pretty well," she answered, with a conscious hesitation, in remembrance of the last half hour, when she had so shamefully treated him to a burst of ill-humour.

"Pretty well, is that all? then I suspect his Penelope has been flirting with some other suitor."

At this chance shot of her father, Penelope, in her old childish fashion, hung her head, and to distract his attention, she handed him a branch of hawthorn freshly cut from the hedge-row, covered thickly with purest white blossoms.

"Smell it, papa," she said, holding it to him close, "it is as fragrant as new-mown hay, on which the sun has shone, and better for you than all M'Evoy's odious medicines."

Her father laughed, smelt it, and pronounced it perfect. "But see, little

one, the primroses are getting yellow
with jealousy, and I will not desert my
favourite colours of gold and green, for
your white thorn, sweet as it is. It is
all too like woman's love, light as air,
and just as fleeting, see how the blossoms fall around me!"

"Treason, treason, papa! treason
to my sex! I never heard you make
such a speech before. I will complain of you to mother, here she
comes."

"Aye, do, let us hear what she
says."

Annie entered, looking not so placid
as usual, nor so Madonna like in her
pure paleness. No! an unaccustomed
flush suffused her cheeks, and a restless
look disturbed the serenity of her eyes.

The facts were Annie was troubled—
and troubled as she never yet had been
save once, perhaps, and then unlike her
present state of feeling, when anger had
predominated over her passion of love.
She has seen Charley once more, the
first time since the despairing parting
he had taken from her at that ball
of nine long years ago; when she
swore to vows—eternal vows of con-
stancy, and broke them within a few
weeks; and never wrote one line to
soothe the wronged heart of that
passionate young fellow. As the wife
of Andrew Jennings how could she?
How should she? But before?—And
now they have met eye to eye, and
what did she see there in that moment
of time? Was it Charley Maitland,

the enthusiastic young man, with blue
eye and open face of her memory and
sometimes of her dreams?—nay, but
Charles Maitland the betrayed—re-
vengeful man—filled with memories
of past days—seared—blasted—lost to
faith in woman—to belief in himself.
Was this indeed her work?

Annie was not accustomed to analy-
zation of causes and effects, and she
grew puzzled. She felt uncomfortable
decidedly, and especially so, whenever she thought of Andrew and remembered that he was her husband.
He had mentioned casually the strange
gentleman whose brandy Doctor M'Evoy
had seized on for him, and Annie,
although she knew well to whom her
husband was indebted for that kindness,

was silent on the subject, and she forbade Penelope to mention before her father the perilous accident they had so nearly met with lest, she said, "It should have a bad effect in his weak state." Prudent, thoughtful Annie—so Penelope was silent and did not hear that her father had met the same carriage, and happily so, since he needed so badly the assistance he received from the stranger.

"Mother, papa deserves a scolding, just hear what he says," and Penelope repeated his criticism on the hawthorn blossom and women.

Doctor Jennings watched for the effect on Annie, she quickly glanced from Penelope to him and met the clear light from his eyes, and there was something so full of meaning in them, yet so vague and uncertain that she quivered under it.

Annie's feelings were deepening, she was beginning to yearn for a love not needed, when offered to her, and to understand also the priceless value of hearts she had so coldly broken, and thought it no sin : remembering them only when she grieved in her cool fashion for the tender looks she received no more. Like to moonlight was Madonna Annie, beautiful in brightness and in light, yet giving out no heat; the warmth her lovers received came from their own bosoms, and they knew it not until experience had taught them the severe lesson.

Annie sought a refuge for her eyes

from her husband's searching gaze in
her ever ready knitting. She sat beside his sofa and plied the ivory needles
over which she bent low that treacherous
head. Doctor Jennings sighed deeply,
then turning to Penelope who was
unusually silent, he asked her for the
Elliots. "Who did you see at Bees
Crag, my pet?"

"Billie and Mrs. Elliot," she answered glibly enough, and then taking
a long breath as if it were an effort she
was making, she knelt beside her
father and began.

"Papa, there are people staying at
Bees Crag now, and it was not all like
itself this morning. The Elliots from
India are there, Colonel Elliot and
Billie's mother, Lady Julia; and

Major Maitland and his little girl, and I saw Major Maitland for a few moments, and he is very handsome, and Colonel Elliot was there also, but I do not remember him."

Annie was not prepared for this; she had guessed Charley Maitland to have been in the country, but she imagined—to her great relief—that he was leaving it when they met yesterday. Now to hear that he was not only so very near to her home, but also to receive the startling announcement that he was married—had a child —to hear all this also at her husband's side—did it not require more self-possession and repression than even Madonna Annie could bring to the emergency?

Doctor Jennings listened intently to the hurried breathless account Penelope gave, and then quickly he turned his eyes to Annie, who involuntarily had let slip the ivory needles from her trembling fingers, and with dilated eyes and burning cheeks was looking at Penelope. Impelled by an irresistible power she turned her terrified face to her husband's, and read there distinctly a full perfect *knowledge* of her treachery—of her guilt—a *knowledge* of the very man to whom she had plighted her troth, and all unredeemed from which, had gone to her friend— her companion of early days—to Andrew Jennings—and had accepted the sacred bonds of his wife. Covering her crimson face with both hands she rose, and fled from the room—fled from the presence of her injured husband, and of his innocent child.

"Is mother ill?" wonderingly inquired Penelope.

"Yes, my darling, I believe so; leave me alone, my child, for a little," he added faintly, and Penelope unsuspecting any serious attack, left him alone.

Alone indeed! save for Him who was near and heard the agonized cry go up, for pity on the man laden with more than he could bear. What was left to him on earth? His duty was fulfilled—but what remained? Where was the reward? Was it then for reward he had laboured? No, truly, in his work and duty fulfilling he was rewarded, and yet he was not happy; the yearning for love—to be beloved, so intense in his nature had not been satisfied; and still craving for it, he was dying with its mocking shadow beneath his roof. Would a mortal love have satisfied this nature? Perhaps not satisfy—the purest earthly love can never quite content the immortal spirit, but the love of a pure-minded woman, self-forgetting, in the very abandonment of her affections, could have made the existence of Andrew Jennings as near blessed as was possible on earth—and Annie Jennings had cursed it.

"Oh God, show me Thyself," went up his anguished cry; "in Thee alone —in purity and righteousness can be peace." And, in the words of the prince who had power and prevailed, he cried again, "I will not let Thee go unless Thou blessest me;" and he was heard.

An hour and more passed, and still there came no summons to that chamber, no ring of the accustomed gong left ready to his hand on the table beside him, and Annie wondered. She stole to his door and knocked—she knocked again, and still no reply—then she crept in, a nameless horrid fear suddenly seizing her. "Andrew," she called and no reply—"Andrew," she louder called, and sprang forward to the sofa on which lay her husband. His head was on the cushions, his hands were folded on his breast, his

eyes were closed—but the beautifully
formed mouth was slightly parted to a
smile—the index of a mind at peace—
the last earthly expression left by the
blessing sent him from on High.

CHAPTER III.

How does she look? how does she bear her loss? is her face red or pale? does she weep much? or is hers a grief that turns the heart to flint and shows a face like to Niobe.

Such questions, and fifty more such, does the world ask after the newly-made widow; with unflagging interest does she repeat herself in making tender inquiries and displaying kindly interest in the every-day occurrence of

a severed pair, whom (it is taken for
granted) God has joined together—and
parted. To the house of mourning the
world hurries, carrying its scales and
weights, and woe be to the woman
who grieves either more or less than
she   sanctions.   Certainly   to   grieve
over measure is the lesser crime, but
it is a crime nevertheless; like to
Shylock, the world cries for its pound
of flesh—and still liker to the righteous
young judge, she will accept neither
more nor less. The widow who wears
out two sets of that mournfullest attire
—a widow's cap, and who draws down
her veil with conspicuous motion when
encountering fellow-men, is judged—
and rightly judged—to be unfeeling—
though not so indecorous as she who

displays her badge of loosened bonds to every passer-by. The world in general judges rightly, for the greater number reach to the bottom of the well and get at Truth—so difficult to find, which the seeker after good values, and which even the bad man admires.

Annie Jennings—Widow Jennings —the widow *de facto* that little Penelope had asserted her so vehemently to be nine years ago, is now become the interest of her little world, and speculations and stories of her are being industriously circulated. Annie is grieved, shocked, stunned by her so unlooked-for loss—for very sudden it came, even to Doctor M'Evoy—who believed Doctor Jennings to be so much recovered that he was actually

on his way back to Edinburgh when
he received a summons to return to
the friend whom he should see no more
in this life to hold sweet converse
with as of old. Ah! how sad was this
return; and Doctor M'Evoy, breathless,
noiseless, crept into the so lately
bright home oppressed by the presence
of the yet unsubdued enemy.

Poor Penelope suffered as a hysterical child does. Her grief was
wild, unbridled, unbelieving; her
terror was extreme, but so great a
loss is felt daily, hourly, and not to
be realized in an instant. For a
little time, poor child, she forgot her
agony in sleep, with nurse M'Laren's
arms round her as if she were an
infant, and all unlike the girl of

that morning whose heart had felt the first sweet disturbance of a woman's love.

That sad night dragged through its weary length to the living friend who watched by the dead friend, and to the new-made widow—a watcher, too, in the sense of one who does not sleep.

Busy was her brain, while thick and fast fell her tears for Andrew—the early friend—the impassioned lover; and for the years of kindness lavished on her by the uncomprehended husband—the kindnesses of a kindly nature—but which showed as years went by, less and less of the love she had taken as her right, and missed only when her power to win it was gone.

Through those hours of waking, the first of her widowhood, Annie's whole life passed in review before her mind's eye, like as it comes to one at point of death; her life's drama was played out in three successive acts of childhood—maidenhood—and wifely state, and each act was closed by death. Was this to be her last act—was her play to be played out in widowhood? Truly this was an early time for such a question, although it was uncalled for, and chidden when it arose in the breast of this new widow. No tangible form indeed did this take, although shadows floated past of old lovers—of a lover now with a child, and whose love was turned to hate—and of a lover unloved, and whom once she had hated, but now remembered with complacency. Was it indeed only yesterday—since she heard of his residing at Callander, and serving the new Episcopal church in its neighbourhood?

But Annie and the other sad inhabitants of the stricken home must bear the burden of the day—the garish day whose sun was excluded as much as closed blinds could effect, and yet was so intolerable. Eating and drinking, and rising and dressing must be all gone through, and it seemed this dismal day to be done for them, the sufferers, as if puppets in some clever manager's hands, who pulled their wires and did with them just as he listed.

Scarcely a sound could be heard in the house, so bright but yesterday;

muffled voices whispered in each other's ears; and Annie, with Penelope's hand clasped in hers, sat beside her bed. In it the poor girl lay flushed and weary, and terribly frightened. "Mother do not leave me," or "Clary, Clary, what is that? I heard some sound," she would tremblingly whisper at times; and nothing stirred in the still house but Doctor M'Evoy's creeping step as he glided from one apartment to another.

Mr. Elliot had called, and had had a long interview with him, and Billie had come as far as the door and trembled so exceedingly that Mr. Elliot would not let him enter. And now Mr. Elliot's visit is over, and the little disturbance made by it is past, and nothing sounds but the scratch, scratch of Doctor M'Evoy's pen. Letters must be written and preparations made for the last sad act left to a mortal to pay another mortal. About this Mr. Elliot had been speaking in the course of that long interview, and he had gone away in consequence of their conversation, disturbed in mind, and feeling very angry with Doctor M'Evoy.

"Tell me, sir, all about those poor things," said good-hearted Mrs. Elliot, hurrying out to meet her husband on his return from the dwelling of the late Doctor Jennings. "How did you find my little pet and the poor widow?"

"I did not see either of them, my

E 2

dear," replied Mr. Elliot, looking more heated with anger than bent with sorrow; "they are bearing up as best they can, poor dears! But I did see that very rough, uncourteous Doctor M'Evoy—how my poor friend, so polished, so courteous, could have selected such a brute—I must call him so, Dorothea, notwithstanding that reproving shake of the head—to be his friend, passes my comprehension. Would you believe it, when I requested permission to read the burial service over our beloved friend, and to bury him in our own little peaceful churchyard, he positively refused to permit it. I argued the point with him—all in vain; I said although the Doctor was nominally a Free kirk member, that he sometimes came to my church, and by his advice his child and wife attended the Episcopalian service whenever they were here; M'Evoy had nothing to say against this, but he repeated like a parrot the same speech, 'I cannot permit it, Mr. Elliot—I really cannot, sir.' Then I suggested waiting until Doctor Jennings' will was opened, to see if in it he had expressed any wishes on the subject."

"Well, sir, what did he answer?" inquired Mrs. Elliot all amazed.

"He said, Dorothea, there was no manner of use, for that Doctor Jennings had told him the contents of the will, and expressly said that he had made no mention as to what he wished with regard to his poor remains."

"Then he must have made all arrangements with M'Evoy, and the poor man is only anxious to carry them into effect. Did you ask him, sir, where he was going to inter him, and what minister was to pay him the last respect?"

"Yes, Dorothea, I did."

"Well, sir."

"The brute said that was his affair not mine; that Jennings' wish was to have no funeral display—*display,* as if my presence at it, or officiating at it, could be a display."

"Very strange indeed, Mr. Elliot. Do you think of trying to see Mrs. Jennings, she might give some explanation of this curious conduct of Doctor M'Evoy; at all events you might let her know your wishes, and your offer about paying respect to her poor husband ?"

Mr. Elliot mused a while, and then said, " I think your idea is a good one, Dorothea; I will think it over."

Mr. Elliot thought it over, and thought so well of it, too, that the next day he rode over to Lunar Lodge, and sent up an earnest request to be admitted by Annie, and in a few moments nurse M'Laren showed him upstairs.

Seated on a straight-back uncomfortable looking chair in a corner of a bedroom not in everyday use, sat the widow, not yet invested with her badge. The apartment was carpetless, the chairs placed *dessus dessous,* bedstead without its furniture, the tables covered with dust. Ah! strange idea to wear grief so, and yet it has within it an element of truth to which our nature unconsciously pays tribute as to sorrow's crown.

Mr. Elliot advanced, and, as in times of grief, the cold proprieties of life are set aside, he ventured on an unconventional step and saluted her soft cheek with fervour. Annie gazed up at him with a startling conviction of a suffered loss brought home to her by his sympathising manner, and also of what was expected from her; and she met the demand promptly by a flow of tears, broken up into showers by attempts to tell how he had died,

of how she had found him dead, and
did not see him die, and how that his
life was now indeed a thing of the
past, and that she was left still to
finish her allotted span in the only
world we know of.

An hour passed by thus, and Annie
felt relieved by talking out the sad
story so shadowy, and strange, that
if Andrew had then entered the apartment, she would not have been shocked,
as if it were indeed an apparition, and
not her husband in the flesh. And
now, before Mr. Elliot takes his leave,
he tells Annie in a few words of his
interview with Doctor M'Evoy, of how
his wishes had been met, and requested
to know if the answer he had received
had her sanction.

"In such case of course, Mrs. Jennings, I shall not urge the matter further, hurt as I confess my feelings must be by such treatment."

"Not another word, dear Mr. Elliot; there must be some great mistake. I will speak to Doctor M'Evoy, and tell him how sure I am that Andrew would have wished to be—to be—(and she sobbed) laid in his resting place by you, and that place to be here—here near to his dear home he loved so well."

"Enough, dear Mrs. Jennings, enough, it shall be done." Then Mr. Elliot took leave and, in so placid a frame of mind that meeting M'Evoy, on the stairs, he shook his hand and hoped he was well, to which courtesy

M'Evoy scarcely replied, and getting very red passed on quickly.

"Queer fish!" soliloquised Mr. Elliot, and then dismissed him from his mind.

When next day Doctor Jennings' will was opened, the contents were found to be very satisfactory to both Mrs. Jennings and the public; for Dr. Jennings, having no near relations, and his wealth being the fruit of his brains, he believed he was just in disposing of it simply in accordance with his desires. He left £10,000 to his daughter, and £2,000 a year to his widow for her life, which at her death should revert to his daughter: and in case of Mrs. Jennings entering into the matrimonial state a second time, she was to forfeit half her income, which his daughter should at once possess; and the remainder as before stated at Mrs. Jennings' death. The rest of Doctor Jennings' large fortune he left to charitable institutions, and to found a surgeons' hall, with which his memory should be for ever associated. A few legacies to personal friends, in which were included Mr. Elliot, Billie, and Doctor M'Evoy wound up the will, in which no mention was made with regard to Doctor Jennings' wishes respecting his funeral.

When this necessary business was got over, at which Mr. Elliot and Billie were present, poor Billie sobbing all through, Mr. Elliot expected that Doctor M'Evoy would address him on the subject of the funeral; instead of which he hurried past him without a word, and out of the room, out of the house, as if he feared being stopped. Mr. Elliot was puzzled, he began to think there must be some mystery; either M'Evoy was deranged, or there were good reasons for his conduct. However, he could do no more but wait patiently for a summons from Mrs. Jennings.

A summons from Mrs. Jennings— poor Annie was not likely to send him such; she sat now in the disconsolate chamber, after having received a visit from Doctor M'Evoy, looking hunted and scared, staring wistfully into the corners of the darkened room. Her hands lay loose in her lap one moment, and the next were wildly clasped over her head, while she exclaimed, "My God!" As Annie did not deserve the name of a pious person, neither was she at all likely to break the third commandment, this exclamation was simply the utterance of terror; an involuntary leaning for protection on a higher power than man.

Now she evidently could bear the solitude and silence no longer, and starting up, she fled to nurse M'Laren's room, which was next Penelope's, and communicated with it by a second door. This was open, and it afforded Annie an inexpressible sense of relief to hear Clary's voice, as she read aloud to Penelope, who lay in bed. Doctor M'Evoy had advised her being kept there for a few days, and Penelope was not unwilling to obey; she felt less desolate in her room with Clary, where she could almost imagine she were a child again, and her father only too occupied to come to her.

Annie sat at the window of the nurse's room and peered behind the blind; she looked out so long as she could see, but blinding tears filled her eyes; she felt what people in sorrow often feel, the want of sympathy that nature displays in our afflictions, she joys truly with our joys, but she smiles when we weep—and Annie closed the blind.

"How shall I tell this dreadful secret to that girl?" she pondered. "It will drive her crazy. Well, at all events, I will wait until all is over, perhaps she won't mind it then—and stay—ah! yes! I have it now, I know what I will do, I will tell all to Billie, and he will break it to her; she will hear it better told by him than by me."

Another day crept slowly by, Annie wrote one little note to Mr. Elliot, as Dr. M'Evoy had begged of her to do. One little note so peculiarly worded that Mr. Elliot was confirmed in his suspicions that there was some mystery connected with the disposal of Doctor Jennings' remains. Annie simply said that she could explain nothing, but she begged him to believe his services, although not accepted, were deeply valued by her.

" Well, sir," said Mrs. Elliot to her

husband, " there is nothing to be done —leave them alone, Mr. Elliot, and take Raby and Billie with you for a canter on the ponies ; the child pines for her father since he and George have gone to that wild Irish coast to hunt seals."

Yes, Lady Julia had permitted the absence of George *Elliot,* called so occasionally even now by her ladyship— she fondly strove to recall him—obtuse fellow—to their sweet early days of courtship, when love was unacknowledged, yet reigned. Unhappy Charley Maitland had proposed the trip, anywhere—anywhere in fact, he desired, so that change of scene, of occupation, should drive away thoughts that were maddening him. All his days of frantic passion for an ideal love were brought back with her presence; and the waste of life, of youth—a youth not to be recalled—caused by her, filled him with wild revenge. It was she who had been guilty of this, and on her head he heaped curses for his reckless course. Yes; she was the guilty one—let the righteous God judge—not he, the victim.

So he and George went to hunt seals; and little Raby was left with Mrs. Elliot and Billie to lisp her prayers for her precious father, with a love inherited from her impassioned mother, a beautiful Circassian, who had followed with untrained purity and faith her love, the careless young Scotchman. Like *the nutbrown maid*, she cared not so she might see his shadow to fall down and worship it, and she followed him whither he went—at first chidden, then suffered, and at last accepted, but without being given the love she coveted.

Among the places he wandered to was the Melanesian settlement in New Zealand, and there the poor Circassian became very ill, and died in giving birth to Raby.

Râ-by, the child of *light,* as good Bishop Patteson had named her in her baptism, and in his care she was left by her father for seven years; and then he went for her and received her from the Bishop's hands, a tender spotless little blossom, knowing nought of evil, filled with love for all about her; and trained to love a father, to whose arms she sprang at sight and adored him, infant though she was, with the maternal instinct of a loving woman's nature. He was to be protected, to be prayed for, the good Bishop had said so, —her first prayer had been for him associated with, "Our Father who art in heaven," and now her every thought centred in him. It was beautiful to see her large grey eyes follow his every motion with anxious loving expression, and her little hand creep into his large brown paw which she would press to her soft cheek and lips.

Charley loved this little crystal drop, yet sometimes her presence oppressed him, like an asthmatic man the air she brought was too pure for him to breathe. How could he think an evil thought, or breathe an impure desire in the very sight of his guardian angel, whose clear innocent eyes looked into his very soul, and yet could not see the dark stains upon it. Mrs. Elliot who had received the child rather unwillingly into her house said to Mr. Elliot,

"Sir, the Lord only knows what kind of marriage a Circassian would require—but the child is innocent at all events—so let her come in Heaven's name."

For Lady Julia had drawn so pretty a picture of Raby, and of her devotion to her father, that Mrs. Elliot's resolution melted like snow at touch of sun, and thus she offered to receive the little mortal to the companionship of her precious Billie.

"Fetch your little girl, Major Maitland," she said, "let me not separate father and child."

CHAPTER IV.

A BOATING PARTY.

STILL as is a house where death
abides, there is always an undercur-
rent of bustle going on, life must
have a finger even in that which it
has lost. Letters are written, letters
are received. Trade is given an im-
petus, it receives large orders—for
respect must be paid to the dead—
servants are turned out in shining new
clothes—carriages receive new ham-
mer-cloths—and relations, the nearest

and the near, appear in sable weeds, wearing the outward show of sorrow.

In the present case, the most interesting of sorrow's trappings is ordered. A widow's dress is in preparation for Annie with the Madonna face.

Doctor M'Evoy receives and answers all inquiries relative to the requests made to attend the funeral of the esteemed physician and friend: all but one—a private letter from the Honourable and Reverend Daniel Merton to the afflicted widow. He is glad to seize the opportunity to renew the old link of friendship with poor Miss Gray's niece, and trusts to death's healing hand to cure wounds he had inflicted long ago. Instinctively he felt that the excuses he could not clothe in language, Annie's own bosom sheltered; the best as well as the worst that could be made for his fierce cruel conduct and contemptuous words.

The Honourable and Reverend Daniel Merton is mortal, and when he read in the *Courant* the announcement of the sudden death of Madonna Annie's husband, the knowledge that she was free to choose again flashed with the speed of light across his mind. At his club in Edinburgh he had read that announcement, and too thorough a Scotchman not to be something of a Calvinist he believed he discovered the finger of Providence in his having just taken the duty of the new church at

Callander. Instinctively he rose and surveyed himself with pleased expression in a mirror—justly he was pleased, and the serene smile which flitted across his rigid lips, expressed the belief that he was a man still to take a woman's fancy.

The Honourable and Reverend Daniel Merton had never looked young, he had been an old baby, an old lad, an old man at thirty—but now was his time for compensation, now the term young could be applied to him (of course, qualified by a " wonderfully young looking man for his years is the Honourable Mr. Merton.") Such remarks he might hear applied to him had anyone ventured on so great familiarity in his hearing.

Mr. Merton, after reflection, decided on writing a letter of sympathy to Miss Gray's niece. Doctor Jennings had attended his mother in her last hours spent on earth, and in gratitude to that memory it was his duty to write to his widow, and in order to recall her to earlier days, to a long-ceased connexion with himself he would with one little touch say a something of "dear Miss Gray, of happy days spent in Broughton Place, Flat No. 3, which he could never forget, notwithstanding the after cloud which obscured their brightness."

Such a letter as is sketched above Mr. Merton wrote, and Annie now read, and read with the feelings he desired. The well remembered precise characters she gazed at, and letting the letter lie before her, she sank into a reverie over past days induced by its contents. How dear Aunt Jane used to treasure every scrap of that formal hand, and place them in the secret recesses of her Davenport. Ah! those days seemed now to have been so happy, when she was petted by that aunt, admired by every gentleman whom she met, when she had had no end of dancing, and when she was not called upon to love beyond her powers. Surely, those were happy days—merry days also—and she smiled as fancy helped her to recall some comical scenes.

She was brought to a sense of her indecorum by the entrance of Mrs.

M‘Laren, who came to announce that
Doctor M‘Evoy wished to speak to
her for a moment. Annie's mirth, if it
can properly be called so, was quickly
spent, and turning very pale she desired
him to enter. She rose to receive him,
but sank back instantly trembling into
her chair.

" Mrs. Jennings, I am very sorry to
distress you, but I must just say one or
two words. Three friends—doctors—
I expect this evening, and then—late
—quite late, I hope all will be over.
I have told M‘Farlane (none of the
other servants), and he has behaved
very properly indeed, and kept down
gossip in the servants' hall. I wished
to let you know this, so that poor
Miss Penelope and you may keep out

of the way. I am very sorry to distress you, madam, (as Annie sobbed hysterically), the business is very, very distressing to me; but not to fulfil his wishes would be worse still! I must see you once again to-morrow morning before I leave this, for a few moments, and then, madam, I will bid you good-bye," and Doctor M'Evoy turned and left the room.

That little gleam of sunshine brought by the Honourable and Reverend Daniel Merton's letter is overcast, and the hours creep gloomily on to evening— to night. Penelope happily falls asleep, and Clary nods beside her.

At the window of her dressing-room sits Annie, and listens to the clock's tick, tick, and as the half hours and hours go round, the hammer falling tells out with emphasis the passing time. Now it beats twelve strokes, and the moon shines with half its power, and Annie's heart throbs so violently she ceases to hear the tick tick from the mantelpiece. Her ear strains painfully to catch any foot moving in that house where servants are in bed, and she wakes because she fears to sleep. A door creaks on its hinges at the end of the corridor where lies in state poor Andrew Jennings. Annie starts, shivers, and draws a shawl closely round her, for warm as is the night her teeth chatter. Now she hears men's carefully lightened steps, and can distinguish the different tread, so as to be able to tell how many

men there are—four she counts, they
all go in, and the door is closed. A
half hour passes, a time appearing
endless to her so great is her nervous
suffering; and again that door creaks
on its opening hinges, and she hears
steps so heavy now they surely must
be carrying something, so stumbling,
yet hurried, is the tread of four men
stepping together; and the door is
closed by one who walks alone sobbing as he goes. That is M'Farlane
she knows, Doctor Jennings' valet,
who had lived with him for twenty
years.

Out of doors she hears that burden
carried, not a step escapes her; on the
gravel the bearers crush their heavy
heels; on they go, more stumbling,

yet more rapid. And now the moon, which had been passing through a mass of cloud, shines out, and Annie sees distinctly what her imagination had before presented to her, four men with their burden wrapped in a cloak. Down to the water's edge they go slipping along, where a boat awaits, into which Doctor M'Evoy (one of the bearers) steps, followed by M'Farlane; and they receive that cloaked form in their arms and lay it down in the bottom of the boat; then the other men scramble in, and push quickly up the loch. On they row with quick, long strokes, and Annie follows them with straining eyes until a bend in the loch hides them from her sight.

With clasped hands and a swim-
ming head that could form no prayer
for the lips to utter, Annie sits, and
the timepiece strikes one o'clock—and
then the silver ring of the half hour
chimes, and simultaneously a red light
shoots up to the sky far—far away
towards the head of the loch. Annie
shrieks faintly, and falling on her
knees, she prays God to have mercy
on his soul (body she probably meant)
—on him who had so outraged the
plan of salvation as to give his body to
be burned instead of leaving it to the
worms; and never thought how guilty
she was just then in praying for the soul
of the departed, a damnable heresy which
her creed condemns. On her knees she
thus remained, unconscious of the length

of time, until the sound of parted water roused her, and, looking up, she saw in the broad light of early morning the boat returning with its lightened freight. All was over— that dreaded deed was done, " ashes to ashes."

With a curious sense of relief, she rose to her feet feeling stiff and cold, and tottering over to a sofa, lay down, drew a counterpane over her, and fell into a sleep—a dreaming sleep of crowding images, the dead and the living, the past and the present strangely jumbled together. They were dreams such as one might suppose a madman would dream, yet Annie was refreshed, and awoke calm and collected to find Clary standing by her side.

Mrs. M'Laren was in despair when she found her mistress had not been to bed that night, and with the tact of a nurse before delivering the message she had come with, she talked triflingly to her.

" A lovely morning, ma'am," and going to the windows, she drew aside the curtains and pulled up the blinds, letting in the sun, which had been excluded from that sad house for six long days. It swept in now with a broad wave of light and shine, not with the frisky playful beams it had danced hither and thither for days before, where all was gloom, and it alone was bright. Annie turned on her side, watched Clary's movements, and knew then that she also knew the smell of death had left that house—it was now the house of the living only, death had snatched its victim and departed. Clary spoke again—

" Doctor M'Evoy, ma'am, saw Miss Penelope this morning, and has ordered her to be constantly in the air; and poor Mr. Billie, who has been breaking his heart to see her, ma'am, has been with her since the doctor sent him up, and the two young creatures have gone out together, poor dears! I am glad of it, the child has gone to a shadow, and her cheeks are as if death had brushed them in passing. Sixteen years old, ma'am, to be left an orphan." With a sudden burst of grief she exclaimed, "the poor, poor Doctor, and for none of us to see the last of him! Doctor M'Evoy tells us it was his wish it should be kept a secret, and so be it! To be sure he was a knowing man, and what he wished should be done, above all his dying desires; so we must not blame Doctor M'Evoy, and, ma'am, he desired me to ask you to see him for one moment—he is going away directly—the other gentlemen have walked on, and the carriage waits for him."

"Doctor M'Evoy," Annie repeated slowly, a disagreeable conviction dawning on her that she had something to go through yet which would be very distasteful.

"Yes, ma'am, for one moment he

says. He has been waiting until you awoke; he would not have you disturbed, but he must leave Callander by the mail day train for Edinburgh."

"Very well, Clary, tell him I shall be with him directly."

At the dining-room door stood Doctor M'Evoy, impatiently, with outside coat on, and hat in one hand; in the other he held something which his coat partly concealed, but which Annie's eyes at once detected and were fascinated by.

"Mrs. Jennings," he began, with a nervous twitch about the corners of his mouth, and shutting the door, "I have scarcely a moment to spare, so I must rather abruptly tell you that all is accomplished as our beloved friend desired, and into your hands I give this," (he drew a silver urn forward), " which I had prepared with inscription—name—and dates all correct, it contains his sacred ashes," and Doctor M'Evoy offered to place it in her hands, but Annie shrunk back with blanched lips, putting her hands behind her.

Doctor M'Evoy was in a great hurry, he could not wait—*Time and Tide*, and to this may be added, *Train, wait for no man*—so finding that Annie would not free his hand, he laid the urn in the very centre of the dinner-table as if it were an epergne, and hastened away.

Annie stood as if rooted to the spot,

and with eyes rivetted on that centre-piece. Her pupils dilated with terror, and her teeth chattered.

" *That* Andrew Jennings! my husband—Penelope's father—the great doctor—the man of science—Edinburgh's pride. Does that urn indeed contain his mortal body?"

It was too much for her understanding, too much for her belief, and she sobbed and laughed wildly by turns. Penelope and Billie, who had just entered the house, heard that awful laugh and turned with scared faces to one another.

"It is Mrs. Jennings' voice," said Billie, "I think she is in the dining-room; come to her, Pen, she must be ill, that is not a natural laugh."

And turning the handle of the door he entered softly, followed by Penelope. Annie turned with quick motion as they appeared, and instantly the fear of Penelope being hurt by the sight of that awful urn drove away her terror, and springing forward she tried to hide it from her view—too late, however, both Penelope's and Billie's eyes had turned from Mrs. Jennings to the object at which she was gazing, and they saw the name inscribed, with solemn wonder.

"Leave me with Billie, dear, I want to speak to him alone," and Penelope, with unwilling steps withdrew.

"Billie," said Mrs. Jennings, speaking in a low tremulous voice, "come here; do you see this urn; it contains my husband's ashes. Yes, Billie," she said excitedly, as Billie uttered a cry, " it was his wish to be burned after death—he told Doctor M'Evoy so. I did not know it; now Mr Elliot will understand how it was we could not accept his offer. This has shocked me inexpressibly—I cannot say how I have suffered; the act appears so un-Christian, and I fear the world will talk. Billie, you are young, but you are grave for your years, and he was very fond of you. What do you think—was it wrong to do so ?"

" Wrong, Mrs. Jennings ?" said poor Billie, bewildered, " no—oh no! how could the act be wrong which he wished done ? And as to the burning, why you know the ancient Greeks and Romans practised it; but Uncle Elliot could talk to you much better than I can. Only I am sure that Doctor Jennings was so very, very good, he could not have desired any wrong or sinful act."

Billie's faith was greater than the widow's, his love *cast out fear*, and he communicated his strength to Annie, she felt less cowardly every moment that they talked together. He promised to break the story to Penelope, to Annie's great relief, for she knew that influenced by Penelope's hysterical nature, her own would be affected.

Billie proposed finding a more suitable place for that sacred urn, and carrying it to the poor doctor's study, followed by Annie, they placed it on the mantelpiece, under an oil painting of Andrew Jennings himself. There it stood, the ashes of the man, looked down on—apparently with approving smile—by that man himself.

Later in the day might be seen poor Penelope kneeling before it with streaming eyes, and beside her with an arm round her waist, knelt Billie, whispering comforting words, believing in his earnest faith, that they three should meet again in perfect bliss, and never more to part.

CHAPTER V.

JENNINGS' WIDOW.

LUNAR LODGE is now deserted. A widow in the first storm of grief must attend to business, when a jointure—and as in this case, a handsome jointure—is attached to the estate; and Annie, *Jennings' widow,* as she is familiarly named, has gone to Edinburgh, to Broughton Place, Flat No. 3, which happens to be vacant now to her great pleasure. Dr. Jennings' town house is to be sold, he ever thought it an unsuitable residence as a private home, and Dr. M'Evoy intends to buy it.

Strangely the world goes round: here is Annie back again in her old home; a widow, a childless mother, with an adopted child, with the experience of the matrimonial state, and free to choose again and to make a good match too—for although she is not in the zenith of her beauty, as compensation she has one thousand pounds a year to give—with herself.

Besides, Annie is still handsome, at times very handsome, as shown so lately when fate would have it that she and her ill-used lover should meet for the first time; and lest he should

not have known her, when fate had
raised the transient blush of her
early beauty at that critical moment,
for Charley to see her a Circe in
unfading witchery.

But some weeks of sorrow worked
a change in poor Annie's appearance, and arrayed now in deepest,
decentest, widow's dress, she also
bears the badge that in childish
fancy Penelope had deemed an indispensable attribute of a widow, *i.e.*,
a tinted nose. Slightly, very slightly
tinted was the extreme point, but
alas! this had become its habitual
tint. Yet our Annie was no wine-
bibber—let no slanderous tongue affirm
it—she was not material in the sense
of loving good eating and drinking;

no, that was not her failing; a
delicate skin was the natural explanation of this colour lodged in the tip
of a rather long nose, ever in the
way of being cut in two by a sharp
east wind, which rather too commonly
blows in fair Scotland.

Mrs. Jennings' mind is more likely
to be turned to hoarding her gold
than to indulging in animal comforts; as
may be thought when it is said that
among other business she had to
transact was that of getting taken
back, by the shop, some fine woollen
vests, bought by her late husband,
and never worn. Improvident, expen-
sive man, to buy no less than eight
vests, made of the very softest and
finest wool; and Annie, looking over

his clothes, and fingering these, guessed them correctly at sixteen shillings each —now, were these to be literally thrown away on Andrew's valet, M'Farlane, to whom thick flannel would be a greater boon? certainly not — and Annie gave the parcel of vests neatly made up, into nurse Clary's unwilling hands to get changed. There was not much else that could be so disposed of, and it was with reluctant feelings she gave over to the valet, coats, waistcoats, boots, &c., as good as new, and all of the very best materials. The handsome silk pocket-handkerchiefs she kept for her own use in case of a sneezing cold, to which affection she was rather subject. Strange it was to see Annie composedly rummage through her dead husband's wardrobe, her temperament being so nervous—yet so it was; give her only broad daylight, and no dark corners, and there are few things she could not do.

Legal businesses are wearisome, in the length of time needful to give them due importance; yet if technical forms were dispensed with — as Latin in writing doctors' prescriptions — both would lose a deal of value in public estimation; for we all like to be humbugged to a certain degree, even when we are partly conscious that we are humbugged.

Constant, almost daily visits, Annie either received from or paid to her man of business. With lowered veil and neatly tucked-up skirts she might be seen walking through the streets, so that not even a speck of dust in that superlatively clean city should touch her handsome crape—and her closely-fitting gloves shewing to advantage the slender hand—and with well-shod feet and ancles, she walked a model widow.

Her mental powers were developing under this new phase of existence, and she who had scarcely known that two and two are four, could now read glibly the rise and fall of stock, and could find the value of any amount of consols at $78\frac{1}{4}$ per cent., if you only gave her a little time.

One day, in the eleventh week of her state of bereavement, Annie was paying her last visit to the office, when coming down the steps, she met coming up them an old acquaintance, with umbrella, slender as of old, and head as erect. The Honourable and Reverend Mr. Merton glanced with the ordinary interest latent in the breast of every unmarried man at sight of a young widow—for decidedly *young* Annie looked, with her slender figure and her veil drawn down; but he started with pleasure when he re-cognised underneath the melancholy veil the never-forgotten features of Madonna Annie. An involuntary ex-clamation escaped him, and he raised his hat; she looked up surprised, and simultaneously their hands met.

" Mrs. Jennings! I did not know that you were in Edinburgh. I came up here yesterday for a few days on business. Where are you staying? May I have the honour of calling ?"

Such information and questions Mr. Merton spoke hurriedly, in some confusion; while his eyes sought in vain the downcast eyes of his companion. Unreproved, he turned with her and walked to the old well-known haunts. Much was not spoken during that short walk, both their minds and hearts were full of dead days, and of dead deeds; of words that had better have never been spoken, of deeds that had better never been done. Yet in that chain of misdoings they found a link that bound them together not unpleasingly.

" Broughton Place, Mr. Merton," said Annie, as he rang the bell for her admittance ; " poor Aunt Jane's old home. I found that No. 3 was vacant just when I wanted apartments in Edinburgh, and I was very pleased to return to them. Will you come in and visit the old rooms."

Mr. Merton was rejoiced to be invited, and ran up the scale stair-case with agility he never displayed in younger days. (It was certainly a physical effort, but not the mental effort it would have been.)

Mr. Merton's feelings were not under the same control as in former days;

he ever had a heart, but hardened by a pride which was more powerful than love, its strength was now diminished; for it was his mother's influence which had sustained it, and since her death he had insensibly softened; besides, he did not need its exercise in any future connection with Annie—*Jennings' widow* with two thousand pounds a year jointure, was a desirable acquaintance for any gentleman.

Mr. Merton's visit extended to an hour's length, and to both Annie and to him it did not seem half an hour. Old days (carefully weeded of dangerous topics) were talked over, and Annie smiled and smiled. She wondered inwardly how she could ever have thought this man stiff, or plain, or old, above all. He looked young, very gentleman-like—to be sure, she had always considered him gentleman-like —very pleasing, and his figure was so nice; six feet high he must be at least; and although perhaps his legs were not symmetrical, they were long and dressed up well, and with the eye of a practised knitter, she unconsciously told off the number of stitches requisite to make him a pair of stockings, and how many rows would be required for their length.

Poor Annie! she felt solitary; she supposed that Charley Maitland was married — in any case he hated her; and she felt solaced in the company of Aunt Jane's old friend, whom she knew had admired her from the first day she made her appearance, *an interesting young person,* in her aunt's pew.

"I return to Lunar Lodge to-morrow, Mr. Merton," she said, as he was about to take his leave; "I shall be glad, for the sake of old days, to see you there whenever it is convenient to you to call."

This was all Mr. Merton could have desired, and, very well pleased, he bowed low over Mrs. Jennings' hand, and withdrew.

Annie walked directly into her bedroom, threw off her bonnet, and surveyed herself in the glass. The tip of her nose *was* red, there was no mistake about it, and her throat was not as full as it should be for beauty's line; but except for these indications of advancing age, Annie had reason to be satisfied, considering that she was not immortal.

" He looks better than ever I remember," she soliloquised; " strange that it should be so."

And Mr. Merton — what were his impressions on seeing her now? In the streets he had thought her bewitching, but alas! when the veil was raised, and he saw the face rather thinned, and the nose rather long and tinted, though ever so slightly, he sighed—that was not Madonna Annie, with the smooth spotless skin, and the look of ineffable purity and repose.

Yet every moment this impression

became fainter; and Annie grew invested in his eyes with a new, a different
sort of beauty. If there was less
repose, there was more animation; if
less purity of colour, more indications
of life. Then Mrs. Jennings' manners
were very good indeed, gracious, hos-
pitable—at least to him; and report
had spoken truth for once, when it
told him that Jennings' widow could
be sold with one thousand a year, if
she . would sell? Would she? and
would she allow him to be the buyer?
These were early days to put such
questions, and in Mr. Merton's mind
they only arose as suggestions. Who
can see a widow without remembering
that she is open to an offer?

This morning was not an eventful

one alone to her. Penelope, walking down Princes Street with Clary, had an adventure likewise. At a hotel door stood a group of gentlemen, and on a very mettlesome horse in the street sat a gentleman, bearded like a pard, and his horse was restless. Penelope, who was very timid, shrank to Clary's side, and looking up at the same moment into the gentleman's face, she instantly recognised, in the careless expression and beautiful eyes, Major Maitland, whom she had not forgotten in all the sorrow that had fallen on her since the morning they had met at Bees Crag. She grew crimson; their eyes met, and with deadly shame she hurried past.

Major Maitland turned round with

an amused look, to stare after the pretty girl whom he had attracted, when the cannon from the Castle Hill exploded, and his horse, rearing up straight, nearly threw him. Penelope saw it, and screamed as the horse rushed past her; then, losing consciousness, she fainted, and was carried by terrified Clary into a shop. Penelope need not to have been so alarmed, Major Maitland was a practised rider, and it required a good deal to throw him off his seat; he simply allowed the poor frightened animal to walk off his terror by a good run, and then rode him back to the hotel to inquire for the screaming girl.

"She is in that shop, Maitland,"

answered one of his friends. "I have just been to ask for her; she is very pretty, poor little dear! even as she lies there, white as a lily. She may be worth looking after, Maitland. I have found out for you who she is—Jennings' daughter, and, they say, with lots of tin."

Major Maitland slightly started, and throwing the reins to a groom, he entered the shop.

"How is the young lady?" he inquired of the shopman, who, grinning, pointed to an inside door, and asked him to walk in. Major Maitland at once went forward, and, to Mrs. M'Laren's great wrath, entered.

Penelope reclined on a sofa, sipping with half-closed eyes some sal-volatile;

her hat lay beside her, and her pretty, russet locks fell in masses round her pale face. At sight of Major Maitland, it was pale no more; half rising, she stammered and burst into tears.

"Please, sir, go away," said Clary, in great distress.

"Yes, ma'am, certainly, in a moment; I happen to know this young lady, Miss Jennings. I met her at Mr. Elliot's house, in the Trossachs, and I wished to make my apologies for having alarmed her. I should have had my horse better in hand," he ended, softly, addressing Penelope, whose tears lessened.

When Mrs. M'Laren heard that the gentleman was Mr. Elliot's friend, she could not send him away.

Taking Penelope's hand he kissed
it gently, saying he could never forgive himself for having caused her
such a fright; and sitting beside her
he talked of Bees Crag—of Billie—
of Mr. and Mrs. Elliot—asked how
soon she was returning home — told
how he had been shooting seals, and
since shooting grouse — and would
shortly take a turn at the partridges
and blackcock—offered her a wing for
her hat; and then rising, told her
she must promise to meet him at
Bees Crag the day after she should
return, " which will it be, let me see,"
he said, reflecting, " in four days
from this; on the fifth day from this
we meet, Miss Penelope;" and in
a lower voice—low as he had spoken

all through — he added something which only reached her ears, and that made her cheeks tingle and her eyes dance.

" *Au revoir !*" and he pressed her rosy palm, leaving Penelope entranced, and Clary in a state of fume and fury.

" Little business had he to tramp in here, with his spurred heels, and his face all covered with hair, and to kiss my child's hand as if he had known her all her life. That's the second fine officer we have had in. I wonder shall we have any more; I will never walk down this public street with you again, Miss Penelope, without the mistress. Never! I don't like this at all! and I am sure Mrs. Jennings would not be pleased."

"Pleased! Clary; what do you mean? as if I could help being frightened; and as to Major Maitland's coming to inquire for me, it would have been very rude and unkind if he had not. But Clary, dear Clary, I think it would be just as well if you did not make a story of this to mother."

"A story, Miss Penelope! I shall only tell the facts, and they are bad enough."

Penelope was not to blame, certainly; she could not help fainting; yet she did not like the prospect of being questioned by her mother about Major Maitland. She had not mentioned that morning's meeting with him at Bees Crag; her father's death was certainly a sufficient reason for this —still she had much rather get Clary's promise to be silent, and she worked so on her devoted nurse, that before they had reached Broughton Place, Flat No. 3, Clary — though it went against her conscience—had given the desired promise.

Next day, the 28th of August, Penelope and Mrs. Jennings left Edinburgh, and commenced their new course of life at Lunar Lodge.

CHAPTER VI.

ANNIE FEELS A JEALOUS PANG.

THREE months had passed away, twelve whole weeks; surely a goodly time to mourn; our Annie may now well appear to her friends in a state of mitigated woe. Mr. Elliot has seen her, and apologised for Mrs. Elliot not calling, but he said,

"She is not very strong; Dorothea is getting into years, Mrs. Jennings! and into flesh too—she has not got your springy step, and she dislikes driving greatly; so she hopes you will kindly excuse her making a formal call, and that you and my sweet little chestnut blossom (so he poetically named Penelope) will come over and dine with us the day after to-morrow, quietly—not a soul but ourselves."

"Dear Mr. Elliot, I don't know how I could do that."

"Why not, my dear friend; remember our long acquaintance. I trust I may add friendship; surely Billie and your child are like brother and sister; and now, except for Lady Julia and little Raby, we are quite alone. My son and Major Maitland are in Edinburgh, and then they are off Heaven knows where. They are always flitting hither and thither, dropping in at unexpected times. The Major, for no other reason, I believe, than to comfort his little treasure, whose very heart is bound up in his, and George—although he denies it—to get extension of leave from Lady Julia. To do her justice, she is behaving uncommonly well, you understand, Mrs. Jennings, but then she has Papa Elliot—as she calls me—to fall back on; besides Billie, who is grateful to be employed by her in any way."

Annie only heard half of this speech; her mind had seized the words, "Major Maitland is in Edinburgh," and again when Mr. Elliot spoke of Raby, how she longed to

ask questions—to know if there was
a Mrs. Maitland, who she had been,
what was she like—was she beautiful,
was she high-born? but she dared not.
She feared lest Mr. Elliot should
know something of her story, and
discover that her interest in that man
was not extinct. How could it be,
indeed? what a woman must she be
who forgets to take an interest in the
lovers, favoured or otherwise, of her
golden youth?

Annie hesitated how to reply to
this warm invitation, and when trying
to frame an excuse, she was stopped by
Mr. Elliot saying—

"Mrs. Jennings, do not, pray,
refuse me. My pride as ambassador
will be dreadfully hurt; besides, I

dare not face Dorothea without your promise to come to us. Say yes, if not for the sake of your friends, for her sake, my little blossom here, who is looking at you so interestedly. There now, I have it," as reluctantly Mrs. Jennings gave the desired promise; "and lest you should claim the privilege of your sex, and change your mind, I will run off. Blossom! will you come with me, and Billie shall see you home again?"

And with the beaming face of one who has accomplished a pleasant purpose, Mr. Elliot departed.

By the loch's sides went Mr. Elliot and the children—as he called them—to Bees Crag, laughing, talking, picking up pebbles and shells, examining

them, then flinging them away,
making sudden divings into the thickets
to look at hidden ferns or mysterious
bits of grasses, for Mr. Elliot was a
dabbler in botany, mineralogy, con-
chology, and all other ologys ever
classed; when their chatter was suddenly checked by the apparition—for
it appeared nothing less in those
wildly beautiful regions — of a well-
dressed polished city gentleman, with
an umbrella all unsuited to bear the
fierce gusts of storms and mists
which commonly arise in those
parts.

No less a well-bred gentleman was
this than the Honourable and Reverend Daniel Merton. He and Mr.
Elliot were slightly acquainted, and

he had just been to call on him at Bees Crag as well as on his cousin, Major Maitland, whom he had not once seen since his return from India, and was now carefully picking his way back by the shore as the shortest way to Lunar Lodge, whither he was bound.

Mr. Merton was becoming daily a more enthusiastic lover of female beauty—the tight hand he had kept on himself in youth was being relaxed; and beware, O, prophet! if the great tension will not now cause a great rebound. Look away from the nymph of fifteen-years-three-quarters, who approaches, with a skin like a sea-gull's wing, and cheeks like young roses; for the time was quickly coming, predicted by her poor father, when his queen would become queen of the roses, abjuring the sole tint of the lilies; and now especially blooming were they freshened by exercise, and the quick breeze from the loch. Instantly Mr. Merton's eyes fell on this vision, and with rather hurried breath, he informed Mr. Elliot of his visit, and of his disappointment in not finding him at home.

"I am very sorry, indeed, Mr. Merton; the Major is absent now, but when he returns you must come and spend a few days with us. By the way," added the impulsive Mr. Elliot, "will you dine with us the day after to-morrow, although neither he nor my son shall be with us, but Mrs. Elliot will be delighted to see you, and I should like you to see the Major's child, the wonderfullest little morsel ever lent to earth."

"Thank you, Mr. Elliot ! I shall be indeed very glad to go to you. Thursday, you say ?—yes. Is this your nephew, Mr. Buchanan," shaking Billie's hand, "and—and—" he added, hesitating, giving Penelope earnest looks.

"Miss Jennings," finished up for him, Mr. Elliot. " My poor friend, Dr. Jennings' only child."

" Mr. Merton—Penelope, my love."

Mr. Merton raised his hat and lowered it slowly to the young beauty, letting her see, with all the power his spectacles could convey, the admiration with which he regarded her.

Penelope liked this and blushed; it was a tribute to charms which she was very anxious to be sure of possessing, for the sake of that fascinating, charming, sweet-voiced, deep-eyed Major. Alas! poor Billie.

"Is Mrs. Jennings at home, may I inquire?" asked Mr. Merton, with suave tones. "I was thinking of calling, if I should not be in her way."

"I don't know," answered Penelope, brusquely; "you can call if you like. Mother was at home when we left," she said, turning to Mr. Elliot with a shamed face. She did not like having to say even so much to that elderly clergyman.

"Well, I shall make an effort at

all events," Mr. Merton replied, not quite so pleased with her manner as with her appearance; and they parted, Mr. Merton carefully stepping on his way.

Mr. Elliot was not quite satisfied at having asked Mr. Merton to dine with him on the day he had promised Mrs. Jennings that there should not be a soul invited; yet the mischief was done. He also knew how his helpmeet, Dorothea, would reproach him; and the poor husband's walk was spoiled; he trudged on in silence, no longer perceptive of Nature's stores.

In a short time, the Honourable Mr. Merton was seated with Annie in Doctor Jennings' pretty home, talking easily and well; Annie knitting peacefully, while Mr. Merton lightly spoke of politics and general social matters, and, without cant or straining even, gave the conversation a religious tone, with which Annie was particularly pleased. He mentioned, casually, having met Miss Jennings, and in a carefully modulated tone of indifference, he inquired her age.

"I suppose she is so young as to make the question not indiscreet, Mrs. Jennings?" and he smiled his rigid smile. (Mr. Merton's rigidity of smile was merely the effect of rigidity of muscle, and for which his nature was not answerable.)

"She is fifteen, I believe," Mr. Merton, not much liking being questioned about her; she fancied, too, that he seemed to attach importance to his query, and a little dryly she replied, which the conscience of the other felt directly, and he changed the conversation.

Lunch being now announced, Mr. Merton, with becoming decorum, handed Mrs. Jennings to the head of her table, and looked around with approbation. Very, very comfortable appeared everything — the table so well furnished; glass so well cleaned (this was a favourite virtue of Mr. Merton's); the massive plate on the sideboard beautifully bright (plate in use always does look bright); a splendid claret-jug and a silver cup, laid (Mrs. Jennings' express orders) beside his plate — a graceful attention from the widow.

"I remember claret was ever your favourite beverage, Mr. Merton," she said. "Are you constant still to your old friend?"

The prophet's heart was touched; that youthful, dazzling vision of fifteen-three-quarters old grew dim, and dimmer still, when Annie had showed him the several reception-rooms, and the fine paintings, and busts, and buhl cabinets, with their valuable collections,—memories from Pagan Rome, and ecclesiastical memories from Christian Rome. He ceased to make comparisons between noses slightly tinted and pure white noses, between slightly rumpled throats and throats

full and fresh, and resolved that no
youthful allurements should interfere
to prevent him and Lunar Lodge
being better acquainted.

In this speculation it would not be
justifiable to consider Mr. Merton sor-
did. He did not want money, he was
perfectly independent — able to select
a beggar for his wife, and maintain
her in every comfort; but the Honourable and Reverend Mr. Merton had
reached that time of life when it is
commendable for a man to consider
his steps, and to get compensation
for his outlay. Money has an affinity
to money; and a rich wife, without
youth and beauty, would be perfectly
lawful for him to take; or, on the
other hand, he might select a beauti-

K 2

ful young wife, even though a beggar, and with her wealth of beauty weigh down the scale he could fill with gold.

Mr. Merton's æsthetic tastes were causing him very pleasurable emotions; but to balance this, the lower nature of the man asserted itself. The claret was really excellent, and Mrs. Jennings' recollection of his predilections was something quite wonderful; this last remembrance kicked youth and beauty clean out of the scale, and Jennings' widow, with one thousand a year and Lunar Lodge, weighted the beam.

Annie looks younger, feels younger, after that visit paid by her old pastor, the shepherd who had rescued her from the Reverend John Bogle's claws, and placed her in his own green pastures. Now, how would she like to become the especial care of that honourable shepherd ?

These were early days, undoubtedly, for such speculation—twelve weeks out of the fifty-two allotted by the world for remembrances of the broken link, and twelve weeks only out of the one hundred and four weeks before the world gives its approving sanction to a broken matrimonial chain being joined with a new link. Yet Annie knew she was in safe hands should she meditate such a joining with Mr. Merton; with him all due regard would be paid to the world's opinion, for, like Brutus—"all knew he was an honourable man."

She knows she shall meet him at Bees Crag, for Mrs. Elliot had insisted on her being told of it, and she had written a note which she gave to Penelope for her, but in which she entreated her not to let this cause her to alter her promise. Mr. Merton, as a clergyman and an old friend, ought really to be welcomed as an addition to their comfort; yet, at the same time, Mrs. Elliot considered she should be left free to draw back if she liked. Annie was troubled; but Penelope's solicitations joined to her own inclinations prevailed, and she yielded.

The intermediate day is one of torrents: a pouring, merciless, pitiless, untiring rain pelts down, mist covers the old mountains, the sky lowers its grey cold curtain on Loch Achray, which looks thick and muddy, and Benvenue, like hooded monk, stands by in gloomy contemplation. The little fishes—poor Doctor Jennings' especial favourites—go sleepily to bed, believing it is night; and in the window, which overlooks the Callander Road, sit Annie and Penelope.

"Mother, I think your old friend is a great beau."

(Fifteen-three-quarters is audacious, and calls fifty odd old.)

"Whom do you mean, Penelope?" demands Mrs. Jennings, with slight

asperity of tone, as *the Blossom* inno-
cently hits on the subject of her con-
templations.

" Mr. Merton, mother."

" How do you mean ? What opportunities have you had for making such
a remark ?"

" Not much, mother; and oh ! please
do not think me vain—but when we
met him yesterday, he looked at me
so — so admiringly — I thought, at
least——"

" Indeed !"

" Yes, mother; and what makes me
feel sure of this was that Billie remarked his manner as well as I, and
asked, ' What business had an old
clergyman to look at me so ?' "

After a pause, Mrs. Jennings asks—

"How old are you, Penelope?"

"Fifteen years and nine months and a week, mother."

How anxious youth is to grow old! Annie is learning a new experience; a sharp feeling of jealousy shoots through her as she gazes on the very pretty girl just bursting into womanhood — such a pain she had never felt before. How can an acknowledged *first* ever feel jealousy?— a peerless beauty, allowed to be so, extolled as such on all sides — what space is there for seeds of jealousy to grow there? Yet seeds there were of vanity, of jealousy, all unknown to Annie until now, and she sighed

deeply. Turning away to hide a painfully troubled face, she drew with
her finger on the dulled window-panes
figures of tall men—of short men (Mrs.
Jennings had a little talent for drawing) of slender women, with cloaks
and bonnets,—of slender girls, with
hats and feathers, and tight-fitting
jackets and Hessian boots,—and she
sighed again more deeply than before.

"Mother, are you ill?" inquired
Penelope, anxiously peering forward
to catch a look at Annie's face; but
Annie impatiently turned away and
left the room. Penelope looked after
her wistfully, but she soon forgot any
fears for Annie's health in counting

that only two days remained before she should see again that bewitching— charming Major Maitland; and blushes and dimples appeared, and chased each other in her pretty cheeks, in remember- ing his honied whispers, heard by no ears but hers. "Heigh ho!" she gaily sighed, and ran to her room to shake out her dress for the dinner next day.

Before retiring to bed that night, Mrs. Jennings stole, with timid ex- pression, to that room which held the urn in which lay the ashes of her departed husband—and locking the door, she took possession of the key. What motive prompted her to this act remains a mystery in the bosom of Annie herself; and each reader is left to imagine what would have been his or her reasons for taking such a step under similar circumstances, and to impute such to our heroine.

CHAPTER VII.

A DINNER.

NEXT morning broke in sunshine and in colour; the brown birds sang, and the flies hummed, and bees buzzed busily, and the fishes leaped high in the clear waters, and Benvenue threw off his cowl and Benedictine cloak, and appeared in secular habit. Annie and Penelope felt a little nervous and anxious, and from similar causes— each thought of Charley Maitland, each of the Honourable and Reverend Mr.

Merton: Penelope, certainly, with more feelings of amusement than of sentiment, yet her vanity was flattered by his speaking looks of admiration and of deference, and in Major Maitland's absence she would not object to playing off a few affected airs on him—it would be such fun! but Annie was realising the old days past, and forestalling in thought prospective ones.

The afternoon was so charming, she resolved to walk quietly by the Loch to Bees Crag. "We will start a little earlier than necessary, to be in time for dinner, Pen," she said, "to permit of delays in the way, should we like to rest." And in full time both ladies started on their expedition. Mrs. Jennings looking the primmest and pro-

perest of widows, closely veiled, cloaked,
and neatly made up for a wet road.

Penelope, although dressed in her
mournful black, looked like nature this
day—fresh—bright—glistening in the
sun—gorgeous and sweet. A tiny
bouquet of scarlet blossom and grey
heliotrope, with a spray of myrtle-
blossom, peeped from her bosom, as
if calling for attention to their resting-
place. And Annie surveyed her with
admiration, but, alas! not without a
pang of jealousy; with a deep sigh she
acknowledged her own lesser charms,
and knew that the first and the best
half of her drama of life was played
out. Penelope bounded before her,
carolling like a lark, after a peep in
at the golden gates, when suddenly she

ceased, as she perceived hastening after them, with hurried yet cautious steps— to avoid pools of water—the Honourable and Reverend Daniel Merton himself. Dimples broke out over her face, and with a merry smile she told Annie that Mr. Merton was on their track. Annie raised her hand with a quick motion to draw down her veil; it was not needed, however—the veil was obscuring quite properly the features of the relict of Andrew Jennings, Esq., M.D., F.R.C.S., and every other letter of the alphabet placed higgledy-piggledy.

"I am fortunate, Mrs. Jennings, to overtake you thus. I trust I am correct in guessing you, like myself, to be on your way to Bees Crag."

"Yes! we dine there to-day, and I understand that you do also."

"Yes! I rejoice to say. Will you accept the support of my arm?— these shingles are slippery walk- ing."

Quite true, so they were, and Annie took the arm thus offered. This was as it should be. Affliction requires a prop, it is supposed to be weakly, and should be treated with considera- tion. Now, there was nothing volatile or frivolous in this act of Annie's taking Mr. Merton's arm; no, on the contrary —and should Mrs. Jennings have met with any friend on the road, she needed not to blush at being seen leaning on the arm of this elderly clergyman, with her young daughter skimming the earth

beside her, for it was not walking with
Penelope this day; and while Mr. Merton's tongue flowed in smooth phrases
to Jennings' widow, his eyes followed,
with delighted glitter, the figure of the
blooming young Penelope. Mrs. Jennings' eyes being chiefly directed to the
ground, did not perceive this, and
Bees Crag was reached this day without fatigue, and with a sense of its
being a very short walk indeed from
Lunar Lodge.

Mrs. Elliot, with all the warm and
hospitality of her good nature, met
Annie on the threshold with outstretched arms.

"Welcome, my poor dear friend,
and thank you very much for coming
to us!" and Mr. Elliot welcomed her with

the gentle salute on her soft cheek, as
he has done since her bereavement.
Annie, quite overcome by their kindness and a general feeling of weakness,
burst into tears, and was led into the
drawing-room by Mrs. Elliot, where
she kissed and soothed her, and
turned Mr. Elliot out of doors to
join Mr. Merton, Penelope, and Billie.

"Leave us, sir!" she said to her
husband; "the poor thing is a little
upset, and no wonder. I will take
her to my own dressing-room pre-
sently, out of Lady Julia's way, and
introduce her to my little pet Raby."

At sound of Raby's name, Annie
looked up, and her tears ceased; she
longed yet dreaded to see this child.

"Yes!" replied Mrs. Elliot to that

look, "she is worth seeing, Mrs. Jennings. I never met with such a little darling; for her sake I am encouraging her father to make this house his home, for the present at all events. I cannot resolve to part with her, and she with reluctance allows him to leave her behind, even when he and George go on shooting parties."

"I should like to see her," said Annie timidly.

"Well, then, dear, come with me quietly upstairs. I do not want you to meet that painted creature of a daughter-in-law of Mr. Elliot's just now; she would be too much for you, until you get a little composed." So saying, Mrs. Elliot took Annie under the arm, carrying in her other hand her bonnet and cloak, of which she had dispossessed her all in a moment, overruling the feeble resistance which was all Annie had to offer at the time.

As they crossed the hall, they saw a little flirting scene enacted, Mr. Merton was making a motion of a bending knee to Penelope, who, with a roguish dimpling face, was letting him take her sprig of myrtle. An angry flush rose to Annie's cheek, but Mrs. Elliot laughed, and whispered, " Never mind her, Mrs. Jennings, she is nothing better than a child; and as to him, he is but an old fool." And unconscious of having committed a great indiscretion, she continued a low laugh until she had reached her dressing-room, and had placed Annie in great state on a sofa. Leaving her alone there, to compose herself, she promised to return in a few moments with Raby.

" *To compose herself!*" surely there was irony in the very sound. Was she not desolate indeed? A husband who had adored her—dead; lost to her in a double sense, lost to her beyond recal. A lover of early days—a distracted—doting lover turned to be her scorner: and the man she had despised, and now permitted to—to what?—(too early Mrs. Jennings to acknowledge even to your fair bosom a lover) —respectfully sympathise with her—she saw with her own eyes—heard with her ears—bowing before and making foolish speeches to her daughter—her

young daughter, scarcely out of the
nursery.

Annie, retire, you are not wanted;
youth will have its way; fifteen years
three quarters and one week would
make a recreant of any modern lover
whose mistress numbered fifteen by
two. Not so indeed the Ancients
thought and acted; Penelope, the faithful wife, had ardent suitors by the
score after the absence of the much
enduring man for twenty years: and
Helen of Troy dazzled all beholders,
seated at Menelaus' board years after
the war which had slain the world
was sung in story.

Softly now the dressing-room door
opens, and in glides a slender little
girl, with rich glossy hair, purple in

its very blackness, and with a skin of the soft tinted brunette shade. Her features are delicate and refined, but in her eyes lay the attraction which no one could resist; these were large lustrous grey eyes, with long black lashes, and whose expression was so holy, so pure that it might be an angel's soul was looking through them unstained by spot of sin, by struggle to be pure.

Annie felt awed by this little mysterious stranger; dressed in a white frock, high to her fair throat, and wanting in coloured sash or bow, such as are deemed indispensable in these days with young and old.

"Come here, my dear," she said rather stiffly. (She hadn't a good manner with children) and holding out her hand; Raby moved quickly to her side, and held up her beautiful mouth to be kissed—the child did not understand hand-shaking, and Annie's lips met hers; there was a something in that kiss, holy as it was, that recalled young Charley's, and with uncontrollable impulse, she clasped her to her heart and burst into tears.

"My darling, my darling!" she cried, and the flood-gates of a stony heart gave way to an innocent child's little holy kiss. Raby looked at her wonderingly. She stroked her cheeks and laid her head on her bosom, as she was accustomed to lay it on her father's, and then looking up into her face, she said in Charley's voice—

"Do not cry, lady! the doctor was very good, and God took him to Heaven to make him quite happy."

Hypocrisy cannot face innocence without a blush; and Annie was greatly relieved at this moment by Mrs. Elliot's entrance to take her down stairs.

"Dinner is ready, Mrs. Jennings, and will be announced in a moment. Come with me, and we will quickly get over the introduction to Lady Julia. Raby, my pet, what should you like to do? Will you go to the dovecote and feed the pigeons for me? they are all tumbling about on the window sill, calling wildly for their supper—hungry

wretches, they are! just like the horse-
leech," she said to Annie, as Raby flew
off to feed them.

"Well, what do you think of my
cherub, Mrs. Jennings?" both ladies
turned to watch Raby out of sight.

"She is lovely, indeed, Mrs. Elliot."

"Yes, lovely and good, and yet the
image of her wilful father in her tricks;
the turn of her head, the tone of her
voice, is as like him as if he were a
child again in her."

Annie coloured, and confusedly she
answered, "yes." Mrs. Elliot remarked
it; but there was no time for comment,
for they had reached the drawing-room,
and introductions must be gone

through. Mr. Elliot meeting Annie at the door, led her over to Lady Julia's sofa, and the introduction was made to her ladyship.

Very much the worse for the wear and tear of an Indian climate was Lady Julia, except for Mdlle. Annette's clever fingers she would have been a spectacle, but ill-ravages were carefully concealed, gaps in gums filled up, streaky hair made perfect, and palpitating bosoms laid on, and all carefully concealed from Raby's eyes by Lady Julia's anxious wishes. She used to say,

" That child's divine eyes I cannot suffer to be distressed by my necessary *petites cosmétiques;* so Annette, hide them; rather ten thousand times let even the Colonel discover them, if an emergency should arise, than that child."

"I regret so much Colonel Elliot's absence, Mrs. Jennings," she commenced; "I fear our little party to-day will be *triste*. Come here, my Billie!" (The boy rushed to her side.) "You must try and fill Colonel Elliot's place to entertain us. Poor papa Elliot and that very gentleman-like Mr. Merton must not be over-burdened with entertaining us four ladies."

"Never mind, Lady Julia! we are equal to the task," answered Mr. Elliot, good-humouredly; and offering his arm to her ladyship, he took her in to dinner. Mr. Merton advanced to the widow, smiling in the consciousness of wearing young beauty's gift in his coat; Annie's eyes glanced to it, but she quickly withdrew them, and spoke in as calm tones as she could command. Billie followed with Penelope, and apparently some sparring passed between them in that short transit, for Billie glared like a young tiger as Mr. Merton seated himself opposite to him, and Miss Penelope demurely looked possessed with a latent desire to laugh.

Very seriously, with due importance given to the acts, were soup and fish eaten and despatched, when Penelope, whose eyes were looking for distraction out of window (to whom the age had not arrived to appreciate any courses but sweet courses,) saw two travel-stained, dusty gentlemen, carrying guns in their cases, pass the windows, and followed by a boy with portmanteau. Her cheeks crimsoned, and Billie, who also saw the arrival, started up, exclaiming :—

"There are Colonel Elliot and Major Maitland."

"I am so rejoiced!" said Lady Julia, turning politely to Annie, who, white as paper, lay back in her chair, trying to look indifferent.

"Desire that the soup and fish be kept hot," said Mrs. Elliot to the servant.

"Confound them!" muttered Mr. Elliot under breath, looking at Annie's white face. "I wish George knew his mind a little better, and would tell us when to expect him and his friends."

Mr. Merton finished his fish. Cold fish is not good—silly of Mr. Elliot to lay down his knife until he has finished his fish. With ladies it is different— they do not always appreciate good things, but Mr. Elliot is quite aware of its value; so Mr. Merton in his secret soul thought, and deferred his uncomfortable feelings at the prospect of facing cousin Charley in Annie's presence until he had consumed the last morsel. Now he looked up, and was struck by the countenances about him. Annie's distress was evident, attributed, of course, to its proper cause by host and hostess, and shared by them who had led her into this company; and Penelope's cheeks were like the damask rose, and her eyes continually sought the door. Mr. Merton addressed her twice, receiving no answer. How can this be? Surely she cannot be disturbed because Colonel Elliot and Major Maitland have arrived; but Billie, who had started out to meet them, now returned, to say that the gentlemen would dine alone, and join the dinner party at dessert.

"Very well!" answered Mr. Elliot, well pleased that Annie should get her dinner quietly over. But dinner was spoiled to Annie—she could not eat, and Penelope could not eat. Lady Julia left the room to embrace her George, saying she would return at dessert course, and not to keep dinner waiting for her. Mrs. Elliot's mind was turned to sending enough of dinner up to those hungry gentlemen, and she watched anxiously the dishes as they were cut: Mr. Elliot's temper, although very good, was quite ruffled at all these interruptions, particularly when he had hoped to have had a nice quiet little dinner for his poor friend's widow, and Mr. Merton, finding no one disposed to converse, sank into silence.

At last this dinner ended, dessert and wines are left and servants withdraw. Lady Julia returns, as she

had promised; and now the door opens
once again, and admits Raby and Major
Maitland, followed by George.

CHAPTER VIII.

OLD WOUNDS BLEED AFRESH.

WITH the sense of sweetness on her lips, caused by the touch of the fresh, pure lips of Charley's infant daughter, and with a strange yearning at her heart, Annie forgot the lapse of time with all her treachery, and leaning forward in her chair, she eagerly met the first look from Major Maitland; then dizzily she heard Mr. Elliot's introduction as he shook him by the hand—" Mrs. Jennings ; Major Maitland."

Very low and deferentially he bowed, and steadily looked her full in the face—a cold, icy look it was, from which was carefully excluded any shade of recognition; then turning from her, he held out a finger to the Honourable and Reverend Mr. Merton, who had left his seat beside the widow, and met him with outstretched hand.

" How do you do, Charley?" with a voice, which betrayed, in its unsteadiness, the embarrassment he did not show in manner.

" How d'ye do, Cousin Dan ?" cooly rejoined Charley. And taking his seat at the table, he drew Raby on his knee, and commenced directly to crack walnuts.

"Who will have walnuts?" he inquired, as if the occupation was so pleasing that he wished to crack 'em all round for the entire company. "Will you, Lady Julia?" and looking up for the first moment he perceived Penelope; for cool as he shewed, that pale-faced man with eyes that burned like coals of fire, was boiling at his heart, and in his excited state of feeling he had overlooked her; but now as shrinking, blushing Penelope met his eyes, he smiled and bowed, and happy little girl was she when he said—

"Miss Jennings, we meet a day before our time."

He remembered it, what bliss ! and the *we, the possessive we,* was so delightful to hear. At once were her deadly fears allayed that he had forgotten her.

" Walnuts, Miss Jennings ?" he asked. And Penelope, who disliked walnuts and loved macaroons, took the walnuts, and rejected the macaroons offered by Billie, who knew her predilection.

" No macaroons, Pen—how is that ?" he inquired, in a whisper.

" How teazing you are !" she answered, in the same under-tone, while she received walnut after walnut, cracked with a quick, sharp report by Major Maitland.

" You eat walnuts, I know, Mrs.

Jennings," said Mr. Elliot to Annie, who timidly answering something which Mr. Elliot supposed to be yes, Major Maitland directly pushed across the dish to him. Annie now knew that the only recognition she should meet from him would be that shewn by his avoidance of her.

His employment gone from him, he leaned back, and stroked Raby's raven hair, and she looked up in his face with her fond, earnest eyes, and laid her lips to his. Annie saw this motion —felt it rather, for she dared not look— and remembering how lately those ripe lips had touched hers, a thrill went through her—of love—of desolation, and a sigh escaped her. Raby, although blest in the paradise of her father's arms, heard that expression of suffering, and slipping from her place, went round to Annie, and climbed to her knees, as she had climbed to her father's, and it was Annie's arms that clasped her now. Bending over Raby's sweet up-turned face, her tears fell quietly down, and in that infant's divine sympathy she felt a kind of peace.

Major Maitland moved uneasily, glanced across the table for a moment, then drew his hand across his brow as if from sudden pain, and plunged into animated talk about deerstalking, which George and Mr. Elliot were discussing. Mrs. Elliot, who was remarking with dismay Mrs. Jennings' tears, here gave the mysterious sign, which is felt

rather than seen by all ladies and at all conceivable distances from one another; and with a great fluttering of garments they rose and left the gentlemen alone.

Major Maitland drew over a bottle of fine old Port quite close to his elbow, and helping himself freely to it he commenced to talk to cousin Dan.

"You wear well, Cousin Dan!"

"Do you think so, Charley?" he answered, glad to be addressed, but feeling rather uncomfortable at the tone Charley assumed. Mr. Elliot and George had drawn together at the upper end of the table, and were talking in earnest, mysterious voices, the fact being that George was explaining as much as he thought it desirable of Charley's connection with Jennings' widow.

"Are you married, Daniel?" superciliously asked Charley of his reverend cousin and former guardian.

"No! surely no! what a strange inquiry!" rather embarrassed, he replied.

"Strange! how? why?"

"Well—because—because I am not a marrying man, have not been, I mean — a — a — of course you should have been made acquainted with it had there been such a fact to communicate."

"Indeed! you are very good. Ah! yes! you know the interest I take in marriages; you say just now that you have not been a marrying man — which, being in the past tense, does not affect the present, or the future, necessarily—for instance, *I have been* a marrying man, and now, thanks to you, I am cured of that weakness; by the way, I should have introduced my daughter to you—you did not know the mother." Mr. Merton grew crimson, an insult to his cloth; " I wonder should you have admired her; but, let me see, I am diverging from the matter in hand. I have been thinking a good deal of you since I returned here, an hour or so ago, and found unexpected company."

" You are very good," drily remarked Mr. Merton, perceiving that Charley expected some reply.

" Yes ! I agree with you. Well, then, I think now is your time for a change of state. Fortune is at your door—pick her up, Cousin Dan ; now what do you say to marrying Jennings' widow ?"

Major Maitland poured out a bumper, and drained it at a gulp, looking fixedly at Mr. Merton's confused face. It was trying to have his contemplated act suggested by another. " Eh, eh !" he stammered.

" Is the prospect not pleasing ? Perhaps she is too old for your youth ? and, I grant you, we don't value the fruit ready to fall at the touch of any hand : even the golden apples

of Hesperides would not be worth
picking-up if they fell liberally; but
there is the daughter—what do you
say to her?"

" Charley, Charley, you are sadly
changed! I fear the stories we have
heard are too true. I had hoped
that they were exaggerated, at least;
but that cold, satirical countenance
and careless lip corroborate them, I
greatly fear. Ah! Charley, what
would my dear mother think, were
she alive to see you, of the change
wrought in the carefully-trained Scotch
lad she parted from so unwillingly ten
years ago!"

" Daniel, cease!" answered Charley,
his manner changing from its satirical
sneering tone, to one of grave severity;

"from you, of all men living, will I suffer no reproof. Who caused this change you complain of? who blasted my life? who turned the honey of my nature to gall and wormwood? Cease, sir, this moment!" and he struck the table till the glasses rang again.

George started, and whispering to his father, they left the cousins alone.

"I know, Charley," said Mr. Merton, firmly, "that you accuse me of this, and I assert I am not answerable for it. I did my duty by you, and what I still believe to have been my duty. Whatever other motives may have mingled in the doing of it, you have nothing to say to them.

I persist in affirming that I acted well and justifiably by you; and, save for your unbridled passions depriving you of all power of reasoning, you would have been obliged to me, for it was apparent to her poor aunt, as to me, that she did not love you as you imagined."

A burning flush rose to Charley's brow.

"You have capped your conduct, sir; and thank your age, your relationship, and your dignity as a priest, that I don't thrash you on the spot for your cold-blooded, insolent taunt."

And Charley started up, towering over the sitting man with a clenched fist, that longed to slap him in the face;

beside him he stood, with his chest heaving with passion; while still as death, and nearly as pale, sat Mr. Merton.

By degrees Charley's breathing became easier, and he said :

"I forgive you, Dan; your old blood runs too slow and cold to comprehend how greatly you have injured me, how much you are maddening me — but hear me—let us two never name this subject again; for I am not master of myself as I should be, when I remember my ill-spent life ;" and Charley, turning again to the wine, drained off a tumbler; then taking cousin Dan by the arm, they entered the drawing-room together.

"Raby is waiting to say good night

to papa," called out Mrs. Elliot, as he entered.

"Not in bed, little one?" he said, stooping over the slender child, who was clinging to him as if they had been parted for days, and gazing into his face with a disturbed, wistful look, out of her great shining eyes. Charley raised her in his arms and carried her off to bed, as was his ordinary custom.

When he returned, in about half an hour, he found his coffee rather cold, and the whist-table laid for the nightly game. Penelope sat alone on a large old-fashioned sofa, placed against the wall, looking rather disconsolate. At the centre table sat Mrs. Jennings, looking very pale, and knitting away with the practised expertness which requires neither eyes nor a present mind to execute faultlessly. Lady Julia stood behind her Georgie, who lay back in an elbow-chair with closed eyes and a newspaper on his knee, and submitted with patience to kisses that she lavished on his forehead and head, laid on from behind. Mr. Merton and Mr. Elliot were taking care of the wood fire and staring at the patient widow; and Billy, very sad-looking, sat at Mrs. Elliot's feet, who gently snored in her chair. The entrance of the Major roused her up, and drowsily rubbing her eyes, she asks Mr. Elliot, won't he begin his game?

"Yes, my dear! so soon as we can

make up our number. Who will play? Of course you will, Dorothea; it is the only thing that keeps you from sleeping in your chair. Lady Julia, you won't desert me, I trust. Georgie, you had best finish your doze." "Yes, sir;"—"and let me see now. Mr. Merton, you will play, I am sure; and, Maitland, how will you amuse yourself? Cut in after me when the first rubber is played, eh?"

"Don't mind me, Mr. Elliot," said Charley; "*here is metal more attractive;*" and he sat down beside the blooming, blushing Penelope.

Mr. Elliot laughed, well pleased to begin his whist, and yet to make his guests all happy.

Very quiet was that drawing-room

after a little; few words were spoken by
the earnest card-players, and Georgie's
gentle breathing, as he lay wrapped
in sweet forgetfulness, was like the hum-
ming of the flies on a summer's day,
making silence still more silent in the
soporific effects it causes. And from
that comfortable sofa proceed only a
murmur, a sweet flow of words, and
then a silence; and Annie's crape
sleeve rubbing against her silken
side, as she plies the needle, is then
heard.

"And so you have been flirting
sadly, Miss Penelope, I find," said
Charley, with one arm thrown at the
back of the sofa, against which Penelope leans.

"How! Why!" she answered, in delicious confusion.

"How! Why! *How*, by giving the Reverend Mr. Merton a flower; and *why*, I cannot say, except that you were then forgetful of your absent friends."

Penelope was desperately uneasy lest the Major should think it possible she should forget him, and so much was she in earnest in her sudden passion for this handsome man, that she did not detect the trifling tone and utter want of feeling in his attentions. She replied vehemently, and with allowable untruthfulness:

"Indeed, Major Maitland, I did not forget you even for a minute; but that old man plagued me so, and made such a point of getting that bit of myrtle, I did not like to refuse it."

"Myrtle? Ah, I see! in the flower language that is love, I believe;" and Major Maitland bent his face down quite close to Penelope's, and in her hurried, upward look, it so happened that Charley felt her lips were soft as they were pretty, and Penelope found that his moustache was quite as silken as it looked. Then his arm would not keep up on that hard-backed sofa, and found, all unseen, a much softer resting-place, and thus happily circumstanced, Charley resumed his disjointed talk.

"So you gave the old gentleman that pretty bit of myrtle."

"Old fool!" ejaculated Miss Pen.

"Oh, Miss Penelope! I am sure my poor aunt turned in her coffin that moment. She thought her son Daniel incomparable."

"I beg your pardon, Major Maitland! I forgot; that is, I did not know that he was your cousin."

"It has not cut me deeply," he answered, smilingly. "Perhaps we agree on that, as I hope we shall do on other matters. Well, (whisper) remember to-morrow. You are bound to meet me to-morrow — this is nothing — a meeting purely accidental. You did not know you were to meet me here this evening."

While whispers like these were in-
terchanged, and some other things,
which, when given, make the givers
richer, Annie worked diligently, suffering torture. Under her eyes Charley
Maitland flirting openly, atrociously,
and with her step-daughter—she did
not know, she could not tell, whether
recklessly or with deliberate malice he
was acting so, for he ignored her
presence. She trembled for Penelope
—the young girl, the dead husband's
darling—and yet she dared not interfere by look or word lest she should
bring an insult on her head.

Billie suffered as well as she; heavily
he sighed as he turned the leaves of

the book, trying to read, and in vain. Now Annie heard Charley suggest their going out of window to look at the clear moon, which was forcing its way into the already well-lighted apartment.

"I want a smoke," he whispered, "and you, like a dear little girl, won't object to it, but will keep me company."

Penelope thought living in the very puff of his smoke would be breathing Heaven's air; and she instantly rose, casting a furtive glance at Mrs. Jennings.

"Penelope, where are you going?" timidly asked Annie, but in a voice that carried no sound as far as Pen's engaged ears; and with Major Maitland following, they two stole behind the curtain, and passed out of the French window.

Minutes dragged slowly on; to Annie's excited fancy appearing trebly long. At last she could bear the strain no more, and, stepping lightly to Colonel Elliot's side, she touched the sleeper quietly on the arm. He awoke instantly, and started up.

"Mrs. Jennings, I beg ten thousand pardons! I believe I have been very rude; I got no sleep—"

"Oh, no matter! I did not think of it," she hurriedly whispered. "I want you to come with me on the terrace. Penelope, and he—"

She stopped, unable to finish; but in a second George understood her and the position of the parties, and offered her his arm.

"Lovely night!" he said, with feigned ease, for he was very uncertain as to how they should find Charley employed. Out of window they stepped together, and there, in the broad light of the moon, they saw — what did they see, but Mrs. Jennings' fears realized—Penelope in the close embrace of Charley Maitland.

"Charley!" cried George, in warning tones, clearing his throat. Charley looked up, still keeping his arms round the girl, and gazing full into Annie's terrified face, he bent back Penelope's head, and kissed her on her ripe lips, parted in consternation as she saw her mother approaching.

CHAPTER IX.

WHEREIN A PROMISE IS BROKEN AND A PROMISE IS KEPT.

WHAT a wretched drive home had these two women, seated by each other's side in the open carriage, with the moon shining its broad smile on the tear-stained face of the young girl, and on the pale set features of the widow. From that moon, which had lightened up the handsome face of Major Maitland, displaying his witchery to the fascinated love-stricken

girl, and had shown her to him in the
glamour of its beams, she would fain
have hidden now; lest the pale, silent
woman by her side should see, though
fear struggled with love in her breast,
that love was triumphing over both it
and shame.

Annie had not spoken a word of
anger to her, yet Penelope's tears
had fallen plentifully. Annie was
suffering,—a gnawing pain was at her
heart, the gentle feelings stirring at
it had received a shock; Charley Maitland had insulted her; with cool pre-
meditated insult, he had injured her
through this girl, her husband's child;
and this girl herself unconsciously
aided in the injury by her *silly forward
love for this bad man.* So Annie's

mind worded it, though not her lips. Angry, very angry, she felt towards her; but beginning to distrust the purity of her feelings, the single righteousness of her anger, she deferred the lecture she meant to give her until the morning. And cold as an iceberg she parted from her at her bedroom door ; Penelope not venturing to kiss her freezing lips—to touch her cold, averted cheek.

"You had best hurry to bed," Annie said, in cutting tones; "these are late hours for a child to keep, and once the excitement of the last few hours has passed off, you will experience an unpleasant reaction."

"Good night, mother," muttered

Penelope, plaintively. She knew she was to blame, infatuated though she was, and determined, too, although unhappy in the thought, to keep her assignation with Major Maitland next day.

In perplexing, happy, and unhappy thoughts she tossed on her pillows that night.

"Meet him I will," was her last resolve, "even though mother should lock me up."

Then, overcome by the fatigue of mind and body, she went to sleep, and went through in her dreams many a sweet word and deed of which she had been the so late recipient. Penelope was young, and sleep is kind to

youth; she enjoyed slumbers, although
shorter than she was used to, while'
Annie lay all night wakeful, unrested.
Her situation was perplexing; of
course, she would keep Penelope as
much as possible out of Major Maitland's way; but Penelope was very
self-willed, she had the passionate
nature of her father, and not like his
in this, her's was all unbridled.

Bees Crag and Lunar Lodge lay
too close together not to afford many
opportunities of the inhabitants often
meeting, and Billie and she were so
used to be almost daily together, that
a sudden change from this habit would
call forth remarks; and she shrank from
speaking of Charley to Mr. and Mrs.

Elliot. Colonel Elliot might assist her in a degree out of her difficulty; for she felt sure that he knew all about her unhappy past connection with Major Maitland, and was also aware of his present dangerous character; and Annie thought she would confide in George. But yet another course remained open—to take Penelope to her bosom and unfold to her all the past; and Major Maitland, seen in the light of her old lover, full of the spirit of revenge — not of love — and trifling with Penelope, simply to heap insult on Annie's head, would surely be a cure. This was a consideration worth something, and Annie revolved it with pain; and then unhappily

o 2

not being able to overcome her natural reserve, she dismissed it altogether.

"I must try soon to talk to Colonel Elliot," she said, "and in the meantime give Penelope a little lecture, besides laying my commands on her not to go to Bees Crag for the next week without my permission."

With this conclusion, so wearily arrived at, Annie was content. She rose with a splitting head-ache, and had to lie down again; but, nevertheless, she could not rest without sending for Penelope, and gently, though very coldly, reproving her for her conduct the past evening. Penelope did not utter a word in justification; her pulse was bounding with pleasure at finding she was getting off so easily. But a few more words must be said before she is permitted to escape from that darkened room.

"Penelope, I must make one request of you, which I expect you will attend to — for one week I desire that you do not enter Bees Crag."

With a great leap, Penelope's heart flew to her mouth, and she stood breathlessly silent.

"Do you hear me, Penelope?" No answer. "I must have your promise before you leave me," Annie reiterated as Penelope made a motion to escape. "I believe you to be a truth-

ful girl, and if you give me your word
that you will not enter Bees Crag
without my permission, I will say
nothing more relative to your improper
behaviour last evening."

Very slowly, very reluctantly, she
answered, " I promise," and slipped
quickly out of her mother's room.
And Annie sank back on her pillows,
satisfied that she might try now to
allay the violent throbbings of her
head.

A torturing ache it was, and becoming worse as day advanced, all
prospect of her being able to stir was
gone. Mrs. M'Laren sat working in
her dressing-room, leaving the door
between it and the bed-room open.

She had no business elsewhere, for Penelope had bolted her door against her, being too much out of sorts for her accustomed chatter with dear old Clary.

"Where is Miss Jennings, Clary?" weakly inquired Annie from her bed, as the shades of evening began to creep over the earth, so bright all day in the glory of a September sun. (Annie had been dozing longer at times than she was aware of.)

"She was in her room early in the day, ma'am, with her door bolted; she would not let me in. I think the poor dear is not very well, for she was a bit sharp in manner, which she never is unless it be owing to that," answered Clary.

"Go and see if she is there, or where she is, and let me know."

In a few moments Clary returned to say she was not in the house. M'Farlane had seen her in the morning run out with her hat on, and he thought she was going to sit in the garden, and did not heed her. "She did not eat a bit of lunch this day either," she added.

Annie, forgetful of her pain, sat up in bed looking alarmed, but muttering: "She promised me, and I never knew her to break her word. Andrew was very particular about that," and she lay back thoughtfully.

"I wish she was home, ma'am," said Clary, anxiously, "though I suppose she is with Mr. Billie at Bees Crag."

"No, Clary, she is not there, I know; if she were, I mean if she might be, it would be all very well. I wonder where she can be. Were there any visitors here to-day? Any of the gentlemen from Bees Crag?" she inquired, as a sudden thought struck her—and she heard with a great sense of relief that no one had been seen in or about the lodge. "She is somewhere in the woods, I daresay; tell M'Farlane to go out directly and search all the places she and Master Billie are in the habit of being in. I

am sure Mr. Billie is with her, Clary
—she is a timid girl, and would
surely not be alone any distance
from home. Go, Clary, and then
return to dress me. I cannot lie
here longer, that child's absence fidgets
me."

And where was Penelope? After
that promise, wrung from her by her
mother, she flew to her bedroom,
and, as Clary stated, bolted the door
and refused her admittance. She
threw open the window, and seat-
ing herself on a low seat, she locked
her arms round her knees, and gazed
out wistfully over the pretty peaceful
loch, to the flower-covered walls which
rose into view on their steep crag.

"There he is!" she talked to herself—"there he is, my own dear, and I cannot—cannot go to meet him! Ah! what will he think of me? He would not take my flowers last evening because—because—" (and at the recollection Pen's eyes overflowed) — "of the myrtle I gave away to that old, detestable, hateful Mr. Merton; and now, perhaps, he will think I do not really care for him, when he finds me faithless to my promises. Oh! I not to care for him—my love, my darling! And I promised to meet him! It was my last word to him yesterday that I would not fail to keep it. What shall I do?" (Penelope wrung her hands in distress.) "That was a promise too, as well as my promise now to mother. Dearest father told me I should always keep my word. Now, in any case, I cannot, and—and—my first promise is the binding one." So Penelope reasoned, but conscience was not satisfied, and would argue with her : "You should have told your mother of that first promise ; besides, you well know that it was a silly promise, and the other—the one made to mother—the real promise to be held sacred."

But, alas! passion is headstrong, and her imagination was excited; the tingling of her palm from the touch of Charley's fingers was still setting her heart athrob, and the recollection

of his sweet, impassioned kisses thrilled
through and through her young frame.
" I cannot, mother!—I cannot keep
my word to you!" she said, wildly,
sinking to her knees in a sort of prayer.
" He expects me—he loves me—and I
love him so dearly! I must see him
to-day! He might be off to-morrow,
and never—return! O Heavens! what
would become of me then! He told
me he never knows, until the day
comes, what he will do that day—and
he asked me to meet him. There
might be something in it; he may
mean to ask me to be his wife this
very day; and if I do not go to him,
he might be so angry as never to ask
me again."

The idea of this was so frightful that she ran to the glass, saw her flushed face and shining eyes, seized her hat, and, without taking gloves or scarf, stole to the door, unbolted it, and creeping down stairs, flew out of the house.

First she went into the garden to avert suspicion, should she be seen by any of the servants—and from it by a path known to few (but to her and Billie), she escaped into the wood that bordered the loch. On she flew, scarce touching the earth, and unconscious of the speed at which she went; and that two mile or so was got over in little more than half-an-hour. And now she reached the forbidden land.

She entered by back ways the precincts of Bees Crag, and panting, exhausted, sank on a bank to rest and reconnoitre. She would fain avoid meeting with Billie—or, indeed, with any one—until she had recovered her ordinary appearance. And Fortune favours her this day. Not a soul is in sight.

She sees the doors and windows lie open as usual, but the garden is deserted. Nobody sits on the garden benches, nobody stands at the windows; no appearance is there of a living soul. Then, to be sure, her view is taken from the back premises;

in front of the house there may be some one.

Rested a little, and wearing something of a less excited look, she now rises and walks very slowly round the house, peering anxiously from window to window, and yet meets no eye. The day is very lovely, and the birds are dropping from twig to twig; squirrels help to break the great silence, and Mr. Elliot's bees are very busy, and tell each other and the world so, with their "Hum! hum!" On Penelope creeps, rustling some leaves. Light as is her step, it disturbs a sleepy man who reclines full stretch on the grass, under a great plane-tree that shelters him from the bright September sun. Penelope sees him, recognises the man she seeks, then with a sudden fear, **turns** and runs swiftly up the hill.

CHAPTER X.

AM I MY BROTHER'S KEEPER?

"AM I my brother's keeper?" angrily asked Charley Maitland of George Elliot, who had been lecturing him on his last night's conduct to Penelope.

"I tell you, George, the girl seeks me, not I her. I have no desire to go after her, and I promise you I won't. Will that content you?"

"No, Charley, it does not content

me. Remember, the girl is little more than a child—scarcely sixteen, I believe. Her father is dead, and here you meet her under my father's roof. Now I would not say one word to you on the subject were she a girl of experience—such a one, for instance, as was Lady Julia (George is not refined), well able to take care of herself. I do entreat you, Charley, to let this silly child alone! Spare her, for poor Jennings' sake. He was a man of uncommon ability, of great kindliness of disposition, and, as a nation, we owe him a debt of gratitude for all that he has accomplished."

"Well," replied Charley, contemplatively, "I promise you, George,

—though I think you a fool to take such thought for any woman—of course," (with a smile, he said,) " Lady Julia always excepted." George gravely accepted the compliment with a bow. " She is a pearl of price. But, remember, should this silly moth singe its wings by wilfully flying into my light, I am not responsible for it. For no living woman will I put myself to any inconvenience ! Bye, bye, old fellow !" And Major Maitland sauntered off, pipe in mouth.

George sighed and shook his head, looking after the retreating figure of the very handsome Charley. He saw clearly that this was a subject on which it was impossible to make any impression on him; and, as he had now done all he could—which he feared was nothing—he went to prepare for a long drive which the entire party were to take, with the exception of Major Maitland. The end proposed in the drive was a visit to a Buchanan relative—but the chief object was to enjoy the lovely scenery on this fine day, through which they must pass to reach their destination.

George Elliot was a very good sort of man—moral, and all that. He went to church, with great regularity, once every Sunday; and if in the morning he were prevented, by having to tie his flies or by any equally important business, he atoned for it in the afternoon by then going to church—and Lady Julia, with reason, was quite satisfied with him. She had never to put on the bearing-rein, or any other implement of torture, to keep him in bounds. No! he jogged patiently by her side through the journey of life, doing great credit to her training.

Charley's conduct last evening had distressed George greatly. He saw how much Annie had suffered by it; and although he had done his best to soften it to her by hinting at what was the fact—that Major Maitland had taken a little too much of Mr. Elliot's good wine—still it had not satisfied her that he had not premeditatedly insulted her through her daughter. With the recollection of her sad, pale face, as he placed her in her carriage that evening, he had tried to exact this promise from Charley, to leave Miss Penelope alone for the future, but with not much success, as has been shown; and Charley was so bored by him, that he was very pleased when he and the rest of the party drove off and left him alone. Alone! until joined by the "silly moth," to which he had likened her, who flew blindly into the destructive light that would so surely singe her.

"Whither so fast, and on so hot a day?" he inquired, gaily, laying a detaining hand on the shoulder of the excited, trembling girl, who shivered with gladness when she met his deep eyes bent on her with dangerous tenderness. " To show yourself, and then to run away! O cruel, cruel Miss Penelope !" And, turning her round, still keeping his hand on her shoulder, he led her under the shade of the plane-tree, and gave her a choice of seats.

"Here was my place, and you can have a seat beside me; the cool, green carpet is big enough for more than us two; or will you sit stiffly up on that seductive iron seat, uncommonly like my good cousin Dan—more pliant than it appears ? By the way, how is cousin Dan ? has he been to see you this morning ?" he asked Penelope, who in a tremor of delicious shyness had seated herself on the grass, while Charley stretched himself as before, and now turned lazily, leaning on his elbow, and gazed up into her down-cast face.

" No, indeed !" then emboldened at the sound of her own voice, she added, " I hate him ! odious, tiresome old man !"

" Oh, Miss Penelope! yet you gave him that beautiful present !"

Penelope looked ready to cry, and, getting crimson, was silent. Charley fixed his eyes steadily on her, and then asked—

" What brought you here to-day ?"

" What brought me here ? Oh ! how can you ask ? Did you not ask me,

and I promised, only late last evening !"
And the threatened shower of tears
fell down her crimson cheeks. What
else could a man do under such circumstances than did Major Maitland
on the spot? He drew her to his breast
and kissed her, and Penelope forgot
her mother, forgot her promise, in re-
joicing that she had come to get such
a welcome.

"Now," thought Major Maitland,
viewing her contemplatively, "since
you are here, what to do with you is
the question. Servants will talk if I
keep you this way."

The entire burden of responsibility
was cast upon him, for Penelope's only
concern had been the thought that

perhaps he did not love her; and now that this idea was done away with by the caress, she remained placid and still in an ecstatic state of bliss. Very puzzled indeed was Major Maitland until a bright thought struck him. He said—

"Do you see those lazy ponies in the field yonder? Suppose we catch them, and ride them over to Silver Strand. Loch Katrine's blue waters would be refreshing this day, and once there, we can capture a boat, and dream a bit on Ellen's Isle—eh? Miss Penelope, do you approve of my scheme?"

Penelope was enchanted; in fact, all places were alike now, so that he

was with her. In a short space of
time ponies were caught and saddled,
and Miss Penelope was placed on one
by the careful hands of the Major, with
a cloak wrapped round her; and then
mounting beside her, they trotted down
the road—the Major's long legs barely
clearing the ground.

Now and again Penelope cast rather
anxious looks behind her, which attracted the attention of her companion,
and he said, with a smile—

"Miss Penelope, do you expect
pursuers? Have you escaped cage-
bars?"

Penelope coloured painfully at the
chance remark, and stammered so in
reply as to awaken suspicion in Major

Maitland ; with a sharpened anxiety, he drew close to her, and with the sweet, low voice, which sent a thrill to her foolish heart, he inquired,

"Miss Penelope do you run risks for me, indeed? Is there a dragon in the the case?" (Poor Annie! Alas! were not days changed for Charley Maitland to designate you, in your maternal cares, by such a name?)

"Oh, Major Maitland! what will you think of me? I broke my promise to mother in meeting you to-day!"

"Ah! indeed!"

"Yes, was I very wrong, Major Maitland?" she inquired imploringly with eyes and tongue; tell-tale eyes

which would have betrayed to less practised men than he the happy story
stirring at her heart.

"Wrong?" he repeated absently; his
mind was rapidly taking in the full bear-
ings of the case, that Annie! his Annie,
his love who had lain on his breast, and
received, well content, his impassioned
vows and echoed them back, should
warn this girl against him! Was it
not enough to have cursed his existence, to burden him with a restless
conscience which would not be stilled
for a ten years' sinful course, without
branding him to her husband's child as
a reprobate? O, heart of stone!—and
Charley's hot blood beat with double
throbs, and the wild spirit of revenge

entered his breast; now, woe! woe! to
Penelope, for on her head shall fall the
punishment due to Annie Jennings'
crimes. No self-restraining hand shall
be held over his passions such as he had
half resolved after hearing George's
pleading reason. No! to the winds let
them drift, Charley Maitland shall do
as he lists this day.

Penelope watched his moody countenance with some anxiety, as on they
rode silently side by side through the
Trossach pass, and round by the sweet
loch's shores, guiding the ponies as
they stumbled tripping over broken
stumps of trees, past broken branches,
past rippling, gurgling brooks with
the deep foliage over head through

which shone the glittering sun, breaking into beautifullest tracery the green leaves. On they rode, Penelope's heart beating restlessly.

This is not like to her mind's picture of lover's rides. Now Silver Strand is reached, and Major Maitland dismounting, fastens the ponies by their bridles to a tree, then turning to Penelope's timid face, he smiles on her a look which dissipates in a moment her fancy's fears that he was angry with her.

"Angry with you, my darling, nay, do not think it, I have been unpardonably absent; but now we are alone in this sweet spot, my little dove shall have no reason to complain."

A lovely spot, indeed, it was which

they two found to sit and bill and coo in—not Eden, as kept by Adam, could have afforded a sweeter place for lover's vows. On lovers such as these, however, the mountains looked down with only half approving looks. Benan and Benvenue changed colour perpetually, sometimes shining bright and gay, then dull and frowning, and the loch looked to share their puzzle, as the shifting clouds over head played at hide and seek with the sun.

Charley Maitland felt to the full the spell-bound influence which lovely nature exerts over our sensuous feelings, and bareheaded he lay back under the young leaves' shade, fanning Penelope's burning cheeks with his broad brimmed hat.

A fisherman dozily sits below in his boat, holding a light line. Charley calls to him, and bargains for an hour's hire of his boat—more profitable use to make of it than the present—and arranging that he should meet them with the ponies at the Trossach end of the loch, he and his young companion step lightly into the boat. Lazy as Charley Maitland looked, he could work energetically at need, and with a few strokes given by his vigorous arms the boat shot soon out of sight, and its owner muttered to himself a few words of Gaelic, ended by a hoarse peal of laughter which was echoed back by the mountains.

An hour or so passed alone with Major Maitland was never beneficial to any girl, to say the least, and if the world could not name his conduct exactly sinful, a higher standard would.

Oh, Charley! Charley! for one woman's falsehood will you punish the race?

But all things must have an end, the sweetest moments perhaps the soonest; and with deeply flushed cheeks and a strange mingled feeling of sweetness and of bitterness, Penelope steps on shore and is lifted to her seat on the poney, with arms reluctant to release her, by Major Maitland.

"Now," he whispers, "for a race through the Trossachs. Our wager shall be—" (the wager is lost in her ear). "Do you agree? I shall not lose in any case. If you reach the entrance first you shall pay me; if, on the contrary, I first arrive, I will pay you; —Agreed?" He placed his ear close to her lips to catch the murmured 'yes,' and they started.

Ponies knowing they were going home, stretch out bravely, obedient to the whip; on they rush through that pretty defile, and Penelope, being the lighter weight, shoots ahead, followed by Major Maitland, looking very excited; but a rumbling sound behind announces the Trossach coach, and his poney getting alarmed, shies, and running up the shelving side, strikes against a projecting oak, then stops terrified. The coach passes quickly by, heedless of a sharp, short scream, which Penelope also hearing, turns round alarmed, and seeing no trace of Major Maitland, she makes quickly back, calling on his name.

No answer did she receive, yet there stood the poney, shivering under a tree, and Major Maitland on her back. Struck by a nameless fear, she shrieks to him to speak. Slowly he turned his head, drawing one hand across his eyes ; then groaning heavily, he fell on the poney in a faint.

"O God ! what shall I do ?" Penelope screamed helplessly as she rushed to his side. But happily help is at hand. A carriage belonging to the Trossach Hotel was passing by empty, save for its driver, who ran to her assistance, and in a few moments Charley's pulse returns, and he staggers to his feet.

"The gentleman will be all right in a moment, Miss," the driver said, kindly, seeing Penelope's intense agony; "just give him a little time to recover."

Charley stood still for a moment, then turning his head from side to side with speechless horror in his face, he tossed out his arms to Heaven, shrieking, "Great God! I'm blind!"

A slender twig, forced out of position in his rapid ride, had rebounded, and striking him across both eyes, was the instrument by which that unhappy man was deprived of the greatest of our Creator's gifts; in one second he was left a mutilated creature, he who was the instant before revelling in the beauty of manhood, and conscious of its power.

When Luther saw the friend at his side struck dead by lightning, he called it the visitation of God —a judgment to be seen and felt by all men; and when Erasmus heard of a powder magazine having destroyed an abode of sin, he asked, why was the house built so near it?

Whether or no Charley Maitland's sins had overtaken him, and that he merited the coroner's verdict of *the visitation of Providence,* is left a question to be decided by those who best understand His ways.

CHAPTER XI.

A HORROR of great darkness, "even
the darkness which may be felt;" such
was the old Egyptians' plague, the vial
of the wrath of the Lord poured out
on the taskmasters of the chosen
people.

O God! the horror of that darkness,
when day is as night, and night be-
comes like day. Surely the Graiæ were

happier than Charley Maitland, those three dread sisters of the Gorgons, for they had one eye among them, and in handing it from one to the other, each sister saw for herself.

The fulness of strength, the pride of comeliness, of what value are these now? Who dare approach that tortured man with vain words of comfort? The ministers of religion? Nay, not so. Mr. Elliot was silent — like to Job's friends, who sat down before him three days and three nights, and uttered not a word in that space; and Mr. Merton—the Honourable and Reverend Daniel—the cousin, the guardian, should not he have had power to pour some balm of Gilead on the wound he *was so sure* a good Providence had made? Alas! no! the priest in the plenitude of his power sank abashed before that great agony, and sat down before him likewise. Job, the pattern of patience, the pattern of affliction, was touched in the flesh, and scraped his sores sitting in dust and ashes, but he could *see* his miserable condition, while Charley! Charley! lay but a spectacle *to be seen* of men. What drop of comfort in that bitter cup had he? Yes; a pure crystal drop from the fountain of divine love —his Raby!

This infant of days, in her love and her faith, in her utter abandonment of self, preserved the tottering balance of his mind, saving him from a maniac's fate. Her cry like King David's rose up, "O! would that I had died for thee!" and day and night she clung in agonized love to the despairing man.

"Away! away from me! I must battle with this great horror."

"Yes; but not alone, father. I will fight with you."

And she prevailed. The loving arms and soft lips of his offspring preserved his latent faith in the goodness of the Creator.

Still poor Charley was quite unapproachable, except by his child and George. George, that faithful friend and wise counsellor, now judged as he thought best for the stricken man, and took him to London to be examined by an oculist, a famous German.

A fortnight passed before this great Doctor would pronounce any opinion on the case, and during that time George arranged poor Charley's future for him. Raby had never ceased a little plaintive cry, "to be taken back to her good Bishop in Melanesia, for he would make her precious father happy;" and although George did not quite understand how this could be, he thought the idea of his going to New Zealand for a time might be probably a very good scheme; the climate was good, and the interest the Bishop of Melanesia had taken in little Raby would be, he was sure, extended to the father in his present state of misery. Charley was utterly passive when George tried to ascertain his wishes.

"I have none," he said, "but to die! to end the intolerable, eternal night of this world."

But a ray of hope remained for the poor fellow. The German oculist at last gave his opinion; one eye, he said, was not quite gone, the nerve had received a great shock, but from which a partial recovery might be anticipated with reason. A bracing climate was essential, and as much hopefulness as could be encouraged, and New Zealand being suggested to him, he approved of it, and dismissed Charley with a cheerful air.

" Keep up heart, Major Maitland! I fully look forward to a partial return of sight. Keep out of England for two or three years, and when you return, if I am still in the flesh, call on me."

And at this cheering news, poor Charley left the room with something of the firm step habitual to him, which showed that the spring of life was only checked in its course—not broken.

And before many days went by a blind young man, holding by the hand a lovely child, might be seen pacing up and down the deck of the Southern Cross, bound for Melanesia.

On a sick bed in Lunar Lodge lay Penelope, the half-heartbroken, nerve-

less girl. After the events of a day
never to be forgotten by her, brain
fever had set in, and for many days
her very life was despaired of. With
a tender care Annie nursed her
through it; and she gained by that
unselfish watching, and the discipline
of poor Charley's great calamity, a
clearer insight into life and her own
state of mind than she had yet ac-
quired. Mr. Merton, too — the Honourable and Reverend Daniel—called
daily to inquire for the sick girl and
the suffering widow.

Not in the spirit of a short time
past, of a forecast wooing of the
widow, and with the admiration of an
old man for a young girl, but in the

spirit of a sympathising friend, of a common brotherhood of suffering, and he met with his reward ; at first, his presence, only endured by Penelope, came to be desired and watched for, and the days he failed to appear were to both mother and daughter unmarked by a white stone.

Billie's nerves had been so over-wrought by the tragic ending to the visitors at Bees Crag, that Mr. Elliot thought it prudent for his mother to take him to a totally different scene, and as this agreed with her own desires to travel, to wander from one continental place to another, she and Colonel Elliot, with Billie, went to Switzerland. Bees Crag was thus left silenter than ever it had been. Mr. and Mrs. Elliot paced it soberly, and their gayest hours were those when letters were brought bearing the stamp of the foreign post towns. No news as yet had come to them of their New Zealand friends, and two years had past.

Mrs. Elliot had a great longing at her heart to hear from that child of whom she had made almost an idol, and frequently she would say :

" Mr. Elliot, sir, I would to the Lord that we had some little word— just a line even—to say that the child was well and happy."

" Happy she is, my dear Dorothea, you may depend upon it, whether in this world or another," one day he answered gravely; "and, my dear, here comes our little post-boy with the bag, coming up the road; let us walk to the gate, and get the letters so many minutes sooner."

Anxiously he unlocked the bag, and the first letter his eyes encountered was a New Zealand one, addressed to Mrs. Elliot. The writing of the address was unknown to her, but the enclosure was written by a child—little Raby's attempt at a letter.

" My Darling, Darling Mrs. Elliot,

" God is very good to us. My father is well and tranquil. Yesterday, I wore a blue ribbon in my hair —he told me it was blue. To-day I played him a trick: I put in a red ribbon instead of it, and I said, 'Papa, you thought my blue ribbon pretty yesterday; does it look as nice to-day?' and only think, he answered quickly, 'My Raby, it looks red to me to-day.' Oh! madam, the joy of that moment; and he is so gentle and patient, and my good bishop loves him."

So little Raby wrote, and characteristically never spoke of herself. But why need she? pure, and true, and holy she is. She sees God now, and must see him hereafter, for the blessing of the pure in heart is hers, and under her purifying influence, Charley

Maitland's blackened soul is coming out white as wool, meet for the enjoyment of the pure in heart.

CHAPTER XII.

CONCLUSION.

WE began our tale with the widow of Doctor Jennings, the celebrated physician, living in her pretty house on the shores of Loch Achray, and we leave her there. She could not be more comfortably or more beautifully situated; yet she feels lonely, and Penelope longs for the day when Billie will return to the loch and become, as of old, her daily companion. That is still a distant day, but it will come.

Billie is busy reading for holy orders, and will return dressed in blackest of suits and whitest of ties, and claim his promised bride, his blooming Penelope— the Queen of the Roses, the poor Doctor's Grecian. They two correspond weekly, and Penelope only remembers her wild flirtation with Charley Maitland as one remembers a painful dream, vivid and yet unsubstantial; and Billie has forgiven her fully, freely, like a noble gentleman, as he is, and loves her devotedly as ever.

The Honourable and Reverend Daniel Merton lives the year through at Callander, having taken on him without hire the serving of its little Episcopalian church; and sees diligently after his few sheep in the wild. These multiply in droves during the summer season, and then indeed Mr. Merton may pronounce with the unction of his younger days, a lawn-sleeve benediction on the fashionable congregation.

Rooms in a farm-house is surely a change from old ancestral mansions in Charlotte Square; and Mr. Merton, although he voluntarily takes the humiliation, casts wistful, almost envious eyes to the pretty abode of the widow of the late Dr. Jennings.

" Too large for a single woman," he was lately heard to say; and report, which told the tale, also said that Mrs. Jennings heard it, and blushed. These blushes, of what were they indicative ?

Had they a significance, or had they none ?   Were they like to sirens' songs, which lure to shipwreck—women have so many wiles ? or were they the result of Master Cupid's paint-brush ?

These are questions to be pondered over, and Mr. Merton is giving them due consideration.   He pays constant visits to Lunar Lodge, where he takes careful observations, and from the manifest perturbations he draws hopeful conclusions.   Surely a crisis is approaching, but in the shifting scenes of life, who can tell the influences which may arise to alter the present position of matters.

Annie has worn out two sets of caps— the widow's badge ; and her friends are

most unwilling that she should wear another cap of the same form. But she
does not like to resign it; clinging to it
with a natural sense of the protection it
affords; and until she decides on other
means of safety, she will probably remain with her Madonna face surrounded
by its halo of white border.

END.

LONDON :
Printed by A. Schulze, 13, Poland Street.

www.ingramcontent.com/pod-product-compliance
Lightning Source LLC
Chambersburg PA
CBHW031427020726

47499CB00005B/1623